Pleasures of Christmas Past
A Christmas Carol
Book 1

Pleasures of Christmas Past
A Christmas Carol
Book 1

BY

LEXI POST

Pleasures of Christmas Past

Summary

When present day American social worker Jessica Thomas is assigned her first case as a spirit guide, she's excited to serve as the Spirit of Christmas Past for her client and prove she knows her profession well. Unfortunately, her mentor, the very hot, very single, and very Scottish Duncan Montgomerie has little faith in her ability and plans to catch her when she falls. As far as she's concerned, he's going to be waiting a very long time.

Bachelor Duncan Montgomerie hails from late 18th century Scotland where he enjoyed life to its fullest, something he continues in death. Having been dead a while, he is well equipped to handle the afterlife where time doesn't exist and phasing is the norm. What has him stymied is his connection to the uptight Jessica and the strange feelings he's experiencing being around her, even though she refuses to listen to his advice. Duncan needs to figure out what it all means and fast because the rules change after death and the path Jessica is headed down could cost her her soul.

Acknowledgments

For Bob Fabich, Sr., the man who showed me exactly how special love can be. And for my sister Paige Wood, who is always there when I need help, even at the last minute.

Thank you to my wonderful friends, Elizabeth and Jimmy Mair of Darvel Scotland, who helped me with important specifics of the area.

Also, thank you to my daughter-in-law Rebecca Curran Fabich who hails from Edinburg. She was so quick to answer all my questions about her beautiful country and helped me with up-to-date information.

As usual, my critique partner, Marie Patrick, was always there to take a phone call and help me brainstorm. I couldn't ask for a better friend.

And I can't close without thanking my editor, Grace Bradley, whose superb knowledge never fails to impress me.

Author's Note

Pleasures of Christmas Past was inspired by *A Christmas Carol* by Charles Dickens. In Dickens' story, Ebenezer Scrooge, a miserly curmudgeon, is told by the spirit of his former business partner, Marley, that he will be visited by three spirits and if he doesn't change his ways he will pay for it in the afterlife. Scrooge scoffs at the idea but as he journeys into his past, present, and future with the spirit of each period of his life, he sees the error of his ways and becomes a completely different man when he wakes up on Christmas day.

But what if the spirit itself, as well as the living human, was in need of help, and the visit could make a difference in the existence of both? Could the Spirit of Christmas Past come to terms with her former life while helping a young woman overcome deep sorrow? And most importantly, can love conquer all even in the afterlife?

Chapter One

Jessica Thomas floated near the ceiling of the small Christmas ornament shop, anxiously waiting to find out who would be her mentor on this, her first case as a Spirit Guide. She had no idea what it would entail, which irritated her a little. When she was alive, she'd been an excellent social worker because she read the case file *before* meeting the client. The Spirit Guide position was very difficult to obtain, but her past expertise had helped her land the job and she was anxious to prove she deserved it.

Having the file would certainly help that.

She scanned the shop, liking the feel of the place. It was cozy, with ornaments everywhere in every conceivable shape and size. With just three days until Christmas the store was full of people, all with lovely Scottish accents. She'd never been to Scotland while alive, though she'd planned a trip once, but had to cancel. She'd just been too busy to take a vacation for any length of time. Yes, it was one of her many regrets she had about her short life. At least *she* felt thirty-three years was short.

As far as time went, her mentor was late, or at least it seemed like it. There was no time in the afterlife, a fact that had thrown her completely off balance, but she was learning to cope…somewhat. Maybe her mentor was still in class answering questions. One of the many instructors from the intensive training she'd gone through would be her mentor on this first assignment. She really liked old Archibald. He was an American from the 1880s. Mrs. Ferrisletter, from 1662 London, was very sweet and would be a lovely mentor. Jessica crossed her fingers. As long as she didn't get Dr. Marley, she'd be happy. That man could put a saint into a depression.

"Are you ready for your first case?" The lilt of a heavy Scottish accent behind her caused her to turn.

Duncan Montgomerie floated there, not close enough to touch, but near enough she caught the whiff of pine that was so much a part of him.

Oh no, not *him*. The man was the hottest instructor she'd had and even now she couldn't remember a word he'd said. She'd been too busy having her libido stroked by his voice while her eyes feasted on his rugged looks and ripped body. He'd never told them what time period he was from, but his accent gave him away as Scottish and some of his vocabulary made her think it might be centuries back, even though he dressed in modern-day clothes.

Nervousness tamped down her excitement. There was no way she'd be able to concentrate on this assignment with him around. She was bound to screw something up.

"Jessica?" His blue eyes sparkled with an unearthly light as one brow rose. "Are you with me, lass?"

"Yes, of course." She tried not to focus on his wavy brown hair that fell past his strong jawline or on his scruffy chin that led the eye to his quirking lips.

His arm stretched out past her as he pointed below them, revealing his forearm muscle flexing as he moved his finger. "That's our case. Mrs. Cameron Douglas."

Despite the butterflies tickling her stomach as Duncan's breath passed by her left ear, Jessica snapped her focus to the people below. There were many women in the shop. Mrs. Douglas could be any of them. She leaned away and looked her mentor in the eyes. "What's her first name?"

"Huh?"

Jessica pushed her glasses back up the bridge of her nose. "What's Mrs. Douglas' first name? To get a client to trust you, you must show an interest in them and knowing the person's first name is the very tip of the iceberg."

Duncan frowned. "I dinna teach you that."

She took a deep breath. "No, you didn't. It's part of the experience I bring to the job. Do you know her first name?"

He shook his head, clearly perplexed by her request.

"How long have you been a Spirit Guide?" It was really none of her business, but she wanted to be sure her mentor was, in fact, more experienced than she was.

He shrugged broad shoulders, drawing her focus back to his build.

"Since we have no time in the afterlife, I cannot tell you how long I've done this, but I can assure you it is no' my first case." He pulled the neck of his t-shirt away from his skin, as if it were too tight.

As far as she was concerned, the entire shirt was too tight with the way it molded to his chest muscles, showing a significant valley down the middle. Hell, if he just wanted to take the whole thing off, she certainly wouldn't complain.

"Holly." Duncan grinned and her insides turned to melting ice cream.

So why did he point out holly? It was Christmas. There was holly everywhere... And mistletoe. Oh, maybe she could find some mistletoe and Mr. Distraction here could catch the hint and kiss her.

"Holly is her first name." Duncan nodded to confirm his statement. "It's also what that older woman down there just called her."

Her? Oh right, the case. Jessica forced her gaze from Duncan and looked below. "Which one is she?"

"She's the owner of the shop. The one with the shoulder-length brown hair and red Christmas hat on."

Jessica forced herself to focus on the woman. Her straight hair was a very deep brown, like dark chocolate, and she had a round face with an adorable smile, but it didn't quite reach her eyes. There was a quiet sorrow about the friendly shop owner. She looked perhaps thirty years old, max. What could have caused such a poignant hurt in one so young? "She definitely has the Christmas spirit. Why does she need us?"

Duncan chuckled, a warm sound that sent pleasure from her heart to her fingertips and everywhere in between. "No' every case is about some old Scrooge character. Each person we're assigned needs something different, but it has to be very important for them. Cameron—he'll be our supervisor on this assignment—received special permission for us to tackle this. You can equate him to Marley in your Scrooge story. There is always a Sprit Guide supervisor who preps the person receiving our help."

"Cameron?" She couldn't resist looking at him again and was surprised to see him frown, an unusual occurrence for him.

"Cameron Douglas is—excuse me—*was* her husband. There is a strict rule about handling personal cases, but I guess Cameron made a good argument with the boss."

Even frowning, Duncan was gorgeous. His cheekbones were strong, but his nose did have a slight bump that kept him from being entirely perfect. Genetics? Or was that from an injury? She could see him modeling for a highland wool sweater catalog, looking scrumptious in a white turtleneck and tartan kilt. Oh. Just the idea of seeing this man in a kilt had her body flushing. What did they say about what a man wore under—

"Jessica? Are you listening?"

"What?" Oh no. She was afraid of this. "Sorry, my mind drifted. What were you saying?"

He studied her for a moment before explaining. "I said, we, or rather you officially, are one of three ghosts who will visit Mrs. Douglas. Our goal is to remind her of the happy times before she lost her husband. Cameron's wife is no' truly living, just going through the motions."

Jessica's heart melted for the woman. She'd had cases like this, but never tackled them with the ability she had now. The possibilities excited her, causing her adrenaline to kick in. "So we literally take her to wonderful moments in her past. This is going to be fun. I can already imagine her smiling and laughing." She couldn't help her own grin at the thought of bringing a client such joy.

Duncan raised his hand. "Hold on, it's no' that simple. Remember what I said in training?"

"Uh, you said a lot. What part?" Not that she remembered any of it.

"You cannot get too attached. You need to keep some distance. We only have one night to work our magic, so to speak." He grinned.

"Do you really believe that?" How could he be a trainer of Spirit Guides if he thought they could do any good staying detached?

His grin faded. "I wouldn't teach it if I dinna believe it. Trust me, lass, you cannot get too involved in someone else's troubles. If you do, your soul will become entangled with your case."

She stared, open-mouthed. Had she really missed how shallow he was in the training? Or maybe he was talking from experience. She studied him closer. Was there something substantial behind those good looks?

His grin returned. "But dinna worry. I'll be there to help." His comment was said with such arrogance that for the first time she found herself not liking him at all.

She wasn't exactly a novice at this. It may be her first case as a

Spirit Guide, but she did have years of experience as a social worker. Maybe she needed to focus on the client and not on Mr. Distraction. "Where's the file?"

"Dinna worry about that. I can give you all the basics." Again he smiled, but this time, she noticed it was the kind a person gives to a child when humoring them.

He had little faith she could accomplish this assignment. Well, he was in for a surprise. She had a mission of her own and that was to prove Duncan Montgomerie was no more than a redundancy on this mission. Pasting on a fake smile, she took charge of *her* case. "I appreciate that, but I'd like to read through the file anyway. Sometimes, as a woman, I can catch a clue or two when trying to better understand a female client."

He shrugged once again and she forced herself to focus on his face.

"I left it on your desk. When you're done looking for *clues*, let me know and we can get started." He was clearly laughing at her.

She gritted her teeth. This wouldn't work. She would have to request another mentor because it was obvious the two of them had radically different ideas about helping people. She forced her jaw to loosen. "Fine." Without another word, she floated through the ceiling and back to her office to plan her attack and have a talk with her new supervisor.

Duncan watched Jessica drift away and chuckled. The lass was "wound too tight," as he'd heard Cameron say. Even her look was too professional. Blonde hair pulled back into a loose ponytail, wire-rimmed glasses hiding very bonny green eyes and a buttoned-to-the-neck Oxford shirt that made her look more like a scholar than a counselor. Her navy-blue pantsuit was boxy, hiding her entire body, and reminded him of a Christmas candle, rectangle bottom with a bright round flame at the top.

There was no way she would get through her first case without messing up. Good thing he was her mentor. He couldn't see any of the other instructors dealing well with her. He dinna doubt her heart was in the right place, but helping the living while dead was very different from helping them while alive.

He had a hard time remembering what it was like no' having the ability to move through space and time at will. It had been so long since he died. He frowned. It was difficult remembering the exact year, but he was confident it was long ago. He'd trained too many recruits. No' that it mattered. Time meant nothing now.

He grinned. Training new Spirit Guides was a fun adventure and he was perfectly happy where he was. It would be entertaining to watch the lass handle her first assignment. And when she stumbled, because she definitely would, he'd be there to catch her. The idea of what she might feel like under all those clothes had his smile widening. First, she needed to lose the glasses and the ponytail. Then he'd be happy to help her change into something more comfortable. Something he would do as soon as this assignment was over. The clothing in his time period was much less confining, but dressing according to the year of the client helped keep the person from running away in pure horror when he showed up.

Activity below caught his attention and his smile faded. He watched their client as Holly helped a teenager choose a unique ornament for his girlfriend.

Cameron and his wife had had one of those rare love stories that deserved a happily forever after, no' just a happily for thirteen months. Duncan had no idea what that was like, but he respected it. To see two people so in love suddenly separated by death touched even his hardened bachelor's soul.

Though he'd only known Cameron for a short while, probably almost a year, it was clear the man was a brilliant supervisor, but like his wife, sadness emanated from his spirit. Holly deserved a wee bit of happiness herself and Cameron could benefit from a little peace. If Duncan could do this small service for him, he would.

And there was no blasted way he would let Miss Jessica Thomas bumble their assignment, bonny eyes or no'.

Jessica closed the file. It wasn't very detailed. She'd expected—hoped—for much more information that would help her understand the Christmas shop owner. She'd bet a gallon of ice cream her supervisor had kept important information out of the file. After all, Holly Douglas was his wife.

The problem was, with so little information, she would be more dependent on Mr. Distraction, a situation she seriously needed to avoid. Between his attitude toward her and their client and his hot physique, it was a recipe for disaster. Not only did she not want that to happen to Holly, but as her client was her new supervisor's wife, she was doubly motivated to do a great job.

Picking up the file, she walked down the hall toward Cameron Douglas' office. She was still more comfortable in a solid state, so she had to knock on his door when she arrived.

"Come in." The Scottish accent reminded her of Duncan.

She opened the door and halted. "Oh, I'm sorry. I didn't know you had someone with you."

Cameron motioned her forward. "No worries." He looked at the woman sitting in the chair before his desk. "You were just leaving, correct?"

The woman rose gracefully. "Yes, I was. Thank you for the advice." Then without turning, she phased and disappeared through the floor.

Jessica hesitated at the woman's disappearance then walked forward.

"Still getting used to phasing?" Cameron smiled encouragingly.

She shook her head. "Not me, but seeing others do it."

"That's normal."

She studied her new boss. He was about her age with sandy-brown hair that fell across his forehead but was cut short above the ears. He had hazel eyes, a narrow nose, and shoulders to rival Duncan Montgomerie's. Despite the sleeveless t-shirt he wore, which made him look like a bouncer, his smile was friendly and not condescending, like another spirit she knew.

"Mr. Douglas, I'm Jessica Thomas. I was assigned your wife's case."

He walked out from behind his desk. "Yes, I know who you are." He reached out his hand. "Call me Cameron. Welcome."

She shook his hand, and when he gestured to the chair recently vacated by the other spirit, she sat. "Thank you. I wanted to talk to you about this case."

He raised his brows at her as if she'd taken him by surprise. "I'm confused. Didn't you discuss it with Duncan?"

His assumption that Duncan had filled her in bothered her. "About Duncan."

Cameron turned and returned to his seat behind his desk. "What about Duncan?" Her boss's smile disappeared.

Not a good sign. "I was wondering if I could be given a different mentor."

"No."

"No? Why not?"

Cameron sat back in his chair. "Duncan is the oldest and best Spirit Guide trainer I have. I chose him because I wanted the best for my wife; however, trainers are not allowed to serve as Spirit Guides, so I chose you out of our new recruits. Duncan is who I want on this case. Would you prefer to be given another one?"

He would take her off his wife's case? That would mean she'd failed before she'd even begun. "No, no. I would like to help your wife. Perhaps you can fill me in a bit more?" She held up the file. "This appears to be a bit sparse."

Cameron leaned forward. "I'm sorry, Jessica, but that's Duncan's job. I have a lot to do here and I assigned you to him to insure this assignment would be handled successfully. So if you don't want another assignment then I suggest you find Duncan and talk to him about my wife's file. That's *his* job."

"Oh, I see." She didn't. Not really.

"Good. I look forward to hearing how well everything goes." Cameron turned his attention back to his desk and started writing on a piece of paper.

Obviously dismissed, Jessica rose and nodded at him, but he didn't look up. Great, not only was she stuck with Mr. Distraction and a file of no information, but she'd pissed off her boss. Good start. She turned and walked toward the door.

"Oh and Jessica."

She spun. "Yes?"

"When you see Duncan, give him a message for me."

"Of course." Maybe this was a chance to redeem herself a bit.

"Tell him my team won and he owes me three beers."

Really? He wanted her to deliver a message about a bet?

He grinned at her, making him look a whole lot younger than she'd first thought. Men.

Too angry to speak, she nodded and turned back to the door, closing it decisively. If he thought she slammed it, that was his interpretation. The chances of her delivering his message were about one in a hundred million. A nagging piece of conscience reminded her he *was* her supervisor. But really, how important could a bet be? Cameron may be her boss, but she wasn't his errand girl.

She skipped going back to her office and headed for home. There had to be another way to learn more about Holly before they started the case. With time at her disposal, she might just have to bop on down to see Holly…without Duncan Montgomerie. Or was that allowed?

~~*~~

Duncan sauntered into Cameron's office and sat, crossing his legs at his ankles. "I have to thank you."

His friend smiled and rose before walking to a side bar. "Scotch?"

Duncan nodded.

Cameron poured a splash of water into two glasses and then filled the glasses three-quarters full. Picking them up, he handed one to Duncan before sitting on the corner of his desk.

Duncan raised his glass. "To women."

"To the right woman."

Duncan grinned at their regular toast and took a sip. There was nothing like good Scotch.

"So what are you thanking me for this time? Did you fall in love with a new recruit?"

Duncan laughed. "No' likely, but I will admit to falling in bed with a couple."

Cameron shook his head. "Two at a time isn't going to find you the one."

Duncan shrugged and looked away. That would never happen. He'd accepted that fact while he was still alive. The truth was, he couldn't love beyond those he'd been born to, like his parents and brother. He just didn't have it in him. "But my new mentee has definite possibilities. She's a bonny one for sure."

"So if it's not love, what do you have to thank me for?"

He grinned again at the memory of his conversation with Jessica Thomas. "Jessica. That woman will be quite the challenge.

It's obvious she thinks she knows what to do and I think she may have slept through my trainings."

Cameron took a sip of his drink. "Funny you should say that. She was just in here asking for a new mentor."

Duncan spit his sip. A bloody waste of liquor. "What? I wasn't even trying to get her into bed yet." His ego as a trainer took the blow hard. "Did she say why she wants a new mentor?"

"No. I wouldn't let her. You're the only one I trust with this visit, so she's stuck with you. You may want to handle her differently than you did. I don't want this assignment screwed up. Maybe you should turn on that legendary charm of yours."

Duncan raised an eyebrow. "I won't let her mess this assignment up. I'll fix her mistakes and everything will go well." He looked his friend in the eye. "Cameron, I won't let anything get in the way of your wife's happiness. You have my word."

His friend and boss looked down at his glass before swirling around the liquid and taking a sizeable gulp. The man's sadness was like a cloud about him. When he brought the glass back down, he continued to stare at it. "I appreciate that. She deserves it."

Duncan took another swallow of his own drink to push down the lump in his throat. He was more determined than ever to help Cameron's wife.

Cameron looked at him. "So what did you do to piss her off?"

He snapped his head up. "I dinna ken."

"Don't know, not ken."

"Blast." He finished off his Scotch. "The language of your time is too harsh." He pulled at the neckline of his t-shirt. "And the clothes are stifling."

Cameron finished his drink and stood. "Holly is used to kilts, so you can change into yours after the first visit or two. I'm hoping your accent and Jessica's experience will put her at ease."

"We will help dispel some of her grief. Dinna worry about that."

Though who would help Cameron was another matter entirely. He smirked to lighten the mood. "I'm sure once I have Jessica bending to my will, all will go according to our plan."

"I don't think she's the type to be told what to do."

Duncan winked. "Then I will just have to woo her to my way of thinking. I have been known to charm a lady or two…or score."

Cameron looked at him quizzically. "Exactly how many women have you had sex with?"

Duncan shrugged before giving his friend a sly look. "Too many to count."

"Get out of here." His boss shook his head and returned to his chair, the paperwork on his desk making Duncan cringe.

"As you wish." He gave his friend a nod before he phased and floated through the roof, Cameron's last question bothering him. Why did he ask?

Duncan would be the first to admit he enjoyed life. At a young age he'd discovered he would never have what Cameron had, though he'd tried, his heart always hoping, but by time he was a score and eight, he'd realized he simply didn't have the ability to love a woman like that.

But there had been more to life than love and he had a brilliant life. That he was able to continue in the afterlife as he had with women, drink and his favorite pastimes was more than he'd hoped for.

And now he had a new woman in his sights. A bonny woman with emerald-green eyes, hair like spun gold, and based on his vast experience, he would wager a cask of single malt Scotch she had a body made for pleasure. Just the thought of kissing her rose-colored lips had him smiling with anticipation. Aye, he was anxious to lie with her and enjoy her feminine attributes.

"Jessica." He even liked her name. It was soft with a hard edge and he'd bet a hundred pounds sterling that was exactly what she was like. He just needed to get beneath that edge.

He hesitated. She'd had a fiancé, which could be an issue. He had to respect her feelings on that. A lover he was, but he'd never come between two people who loved each other like Cameron and Holly.

He continued floating toward home. He didn't like that she'd requested someone else. He'd been very patient with her. Maybe that was too subtle for her. Aye, that made sense. His best approach now was to be obvious. He would charm her into enjoying herself a bit with him, then they could work together to help Holly.

A new energy surged through him at the prospect of his challenge and he grinned. He couldn't wait to discover every enjoyable nuance of Jessica's being.

Holly Douglas closed the safe then turned off the lamp on her desk. It had been a long day of customers. As usual, Christmas Eve had seen her store packed from open to close and for the third year in a row, Mr. Branson had shown up just as she was about to lock the door. He took his usual half hour picking out the perfect ornament for his wife. It had to be an ornament with motion involved. He said it was because now that his wife had a scooter and electric wheelchair, she moved around even more than when she was younger.

She had to agree with the man. Mrs. Branson did seem to be out and about a lot more since she'd finally given up the walker two years ago. She would love the singing cardinal with the flapping wings he'd bought her. Holly could almost picture the older woman opening the gift-wrapped box. Of course, she had been so tired she'd cut the ribbon too short and had to start over. But it was a "holiday tired" as Cam always said.

She smiled sadly as she turned off the lights in the little shop and walked around her ceramic ornament display to the tapestry that hid the door to her home next door. It'd been *their* home just last year.

When everyone heard about Cam's accident, they had been so kind, visiting her every day, bringing her food and company. Later, people invited her to watch the Old Firm Derby between the Rangers and the Celtic or to come to a local ceilidh. But as the year wore on, people became too busy with their own lives and their own challenges.

Except for Cam's two best friends. Ethan and Brody had both remembered her. Brody had invited her to his flat where he was holding a Christmas Eve party with all their friends. Ethan had invited her to his parents' house for Christmas day. Their invitations were just like them, completely different. Brody was like Cam, always ready to jump into another adventure while Ethan was cautious, weighing all the pros and cons before making a decision, yet the three of them had been inseparable since their university days.

She turned both offers down. She had a feeling they both sensed her hesitation to be around them. They reminded her too much of Cam and the good times they all had together. To be in their presence would be torture without him there.

She flicked the switch as she entered her little home. Mac jumped off the couch and stretched his feline body by digging his claws into the area rug before sauntering over to say hello.

"Did you miss me, sweetie?"

The cat insistently rubbed against her leg, arching his back as she gave him the mandatory stroke.

"Well, I didn't have time to miss you. We were so busy today." She moved to the side table by the door and dropped her keys. As she looked up into the mirror above it, she froze. Her late husband stood behind her. "Cam?"

She spun around, her heart beating a tattoo, but no one was there. She looked back at the mirror. Just her round face flushed by her scare stared back at her. "Good job, Holly, now you're seeing things."

With her adrenaline pumping overtime, she took a couple calming breaths and walked into the kitchen. It was nothing a cup of tea couldn't soothe. She switched on the electric tea kettle and opened the refrigerator. She scanned the contents, ignoring the little Cornish hen she'd bought to cook for dinner the next day, and instead stared at the clootie dumpling Mrs. Bell had dropped off the day before. "That's not exactly Christmas Eve dinner."

Mac ignored her as he munched on his own dry food, his teeth crunching down on the hard pellets.

She dug deep for her willpower and forced her hand to move past the dessert to the container of leftover pasta from the night before. Scooping some onto a plate, she set it in the microwave for a minute.

Her family back in New Hampshire had pressured her to visit during the holidays. They didn't want her to be alone so far away, but she just couldn't bring herself to leave. Cam loved Christmas so much. To not be here where they had celebrated their only two Christmases as a married couple had just felt wrong. But her family wouldn't have understood, so she told them she couldn't get anyone to cover her shop. It was actually *their* shop. Cam had come up with the idea and the name "One of a Kind Christmas Shop." She'd just implemented it. It was his brain child. The only child they had. Her living link to him…sort of.

The microwave binged, keeping her from going down the dark path her thoughts always traveled when remembering her late husband.

Pulling out her dinner, she set it on the table before pouring the hot water over a tea bag and letting it steep while she ate. When she was finished with her meal, she made her tea and headed into the parlor to turn on the Christmas lights. Setting her cup on the end table next to her comfy recliner, she went about flipping all the switches.

Finally, she turned on the gas fireplace. Walking back to her chair, she stared down at Mac, curled into a large ball in the middle of the cushion. "I don't think so." She bent over him. "You're not fooling anybody. I know you're not sleeping."

The cat didn't move a muscle, so she reached over and lifted her mug from the coaster. The cat's ear twitched toward the sound. "I knew it." Putting her cup back down, she picked him up and deposited him on Cam's chair. "That's your chair. You inherited it from Cam, so enjoy it."

Once comfortable in her own spot, Holly took a sip of tea and critically reviewed her Christmas display. Just because Cam wasn't with her anymore, didn't mean she should change their decorating tradition. Ever since their first Christmas Eve five years earlier, they'd always decorated the main living room to the max. They'd both thought the same thing when they found this house three years ago, which was that with a ceiling so high, like in their shop next door, it meant lots of room for decorations. The room glowed with a pink hue from all the lights, while the firelight kept it moving.

The flames weren't the only things moving. She had the electric train going around the tree, the various motion ornaments she'd kept instead of selling in the shop, and of course the blinking lights. Some moved in a continuous pattern, others stopped and started, and some simply changed from one color to the next. Her Santa's Workshop on the bookcase was busy with elves working and even the electric candles in the windows flickered. There was only one thing missing to complete the decorated room. The star.

She looked up at the top of the tree where the twelve-inch star belonged. Cam always placed the star on top. She'd tried every night for two weeks to put it up there, but started crying every time, so she gave up. She even put it back in its box and returned it to the closet.

The fact was, she could pretend all she wanted, but Cam wasn't here for Christmas. The room was his shrine, but he would never see it.

Holly's chest tightened and she tried to take a deep breath to stop the inevitable tears, but it was no use. It just made her cough as her nose started to run. Why couldn't she get through just one night without crying?

Because half her heart was buried six feet under.

The pain in her chest intensified and she doubled over, the sobbing starting all over again. Even as the tears flowed, her heart filled with hurt until she couldn't breathe. If she'd known this would happen, this was how it would all turn out, she would never have smiled at Cameron Douglas that fateful day at the Highland Games in Lincoln.

Irritation raced through her veins. How could he die on her? He was only thirty-two. She felt robbed, cheated, betrayed. Holly sat upright as her chest eased but her stomach tensed with anger. She grabbed a tissue from the box on the end table, mad at Cam and at herself.

"Don't cry, love."

Chapter Two

At her husband's voice, Holly stilled, swallowing the hiccup that threatened to interrupt the silence.

"I can't stand to see you so sad."

She turned her head toward the Christmas tree and blinked. Cameron Douglas stood in front of it in his blue- green-and-white kilt with love shinning in his eyes.

"Cam?" Her heart leapt with joy and she flew from the chair to hug him and found herself in the Christmas tree instead, a glass angel ornament digging into her cheek. Righting herself, she disengaged her hair from a reindeer before turning around, sure she would see an empty room…but it wasn't.

Cameron Douglas stood in front of his chair in the Douglas kilt, forest-green sleeveless t-shirt and black army boots, his sandy-brown hair falling just below his ears and a sad smile on his face. Holly crossed her arms to hide the erratic beat of her heart as a shiver raced up her spine. Fear and happiness fought inside her. "What are you doing here?"

Cam brushed his hair from his forehead, a sure sign he was out of his element, whatever that element was. "I need your help, Holly."

She shook her head, still trying to believe she spoke to her dead husband, emphasis on *dead*. "I'm dreaming." She pinched herself. "Ow."

"No, you're not. I know this is a shock."

She raised an eyebrow. "You think?"

He grinned. "Ach, but a pleasant one, I hope."

She relaxed a little at his smile. It was so him. "How come I can see you? You're supposed to be dead."

He grimaced. "I am. I'm sorry. I was stupid. We should have had our whole lives to grow old together."

"You've got that right. But how can you be here? You look like you did when you were alive except…" Her fall into the Christmas tree had her pausing. "Except you aren't solid. It's not fair, you look solid and you smell so good." Her eyes started to water again.

"Ah, please don't cry, hen. I only came because I thought you might be strong enough to handle it. If I'm just making you cry, I'll leave."

Fear raced from her brain to every tiny blood vessel. "No! No, I'm okay. I cry whether you're here or not and I'd much rather be able to see you." She tried to smile, but her lips barely moved upward.

"That's my girl. I knew I could count on you."

She uncrossed her arms and wiped her face on the sleeve of her sweater. Just then Mac jumped down from the chair and started to rub against Cam's legs for attention. "Hey, how come he can touch you?"

Cam's eyes widened before his grin returned. "I have no idea." He bent and gave the demanding feline a scratch behind his ears, starting the purr machine up full blast.

She rolled her eyes. "Really?"

He straightened and shrugged. "I'll have to figure that out later. I've come to ask for your help with a spirit who kind of works for me."

She raised her eyebrow again. "Works for you? I thought heaven was all pleasure and no work."

Cam looked away. "It's complicated. Suffice it to say, I'm trying to help other spirits right now and this one is a sad case."

She folded her arms across her chest again, trying to pretend she wasn't talking to Cam's spirit. "Why?"

He floated to the fireplace, reminding her of his spirit state and completely ruining her self-imposed pretend session that he was real.

"She has many deep regrets."

Well, she could certainly relate to that. There had been so many things she and Cam had planned to do but put off because they were trying to make the shop a success or because they wanted to be in a financially good spot first, like having a baby. Her eyes started to water again.

"Holly? Are you sure you don't want me to leave?" He'd floated closer to her. So close, she could see the different colors in his hazel eyes.

She couldn't resist and lifted her hand to touch his face. As her fingers glided through air, his eyes revealed his own anguish.

"I miss you, love."

She gazed at him, her throat closing off any possibility of speech.

He finally looked away. "Maybe this wasn't such a good idea." He turned back to the fireplace, tension in his frame revealing as much as his eyes. He was in pain too.

Knowing he hurt as much from their separation as she did eased her heart in a strange way, but it also confirmed for her that she'd still do anything for him. Desperate to help, she moved to stand next to him. "What can I do?"

He looked down at her and the depth of self-loathing she caught in his eyes stilled her heart, but it was gone so fast, she wasn't sure she'd really seen it.

"You have the biggest heart, lass."

She smiled a real smile this time. "You always said that, but if you'd seen the way I treated Sofia Dunlap last week, you might reconsider my aid."

He turned toward her and grinned. "I know you could never really do anything hateful, which is why I thought of you in regards to Jessica."

Holly stiffened. "Wait a minute. You said she is a female spirit. I'm not sure I like that."

"Ach, don't worry. She'll have her mentor with her, Duncan Montgomerie. Whether he appears to you or not is his choice. But Jessica is the one I'm most concerned with."

Relieved Jessica had a man watching her, Holly relaxed despite how off-the-wall her flash of jealousy toward a ghost was. "You said she has strong regrets?"

"Yes." Cameron seemed to notice the room for the first time. He stopped in front of a rocking horse that rocked nonstop from a tree branch. "This is new."

She nodded though she stood behind him. She'd added a number of decorations. Probably compensating for Cam's absence.

He continued his walk around the tree. When he came back to her, his admiration shone in his eyes. "It's beautiful, Holly."

She flushed. Too happy he was pleased. "I didn't want to forget what we had."

He scowled. "Don't." His face lightened. "You won't. What we had was stronger than death."

She opened her mouth to respond but the grandfather clock in the middle of the room started to strike ten.

"Love, I lost track of the time. I have to go."

"No." She didn't want him to leave, perfectly happy if he wanted to haunt her for the rest of her days. "What about Jessica?"

He started to fade. "She'll be here at eleven. Just go along with her. She thinks she's helping you, so don't tell her what I told you."

"Cam, wait. Will I see you again?"

His form was almost completely gone, but he moved his head.

It looked like he nodded, but she wasn't sure. Maybe she could ask this Jessica.

Holy crap, she'd just agreed to be visited by a strange ghost! Her whole body started to shake. She had to sit down. Unfortunately, Mac was back on her chair, so she threw her hands up and plopped into Cam's.

His clove scent still permeated the recliner and she inhaled deeply. Her eyes flew open. Was it the chair or his ghost? Turning her head, she sniffed the soft brown cloth. Hmmm, it was the chair. She hadn't sat in it since the day after he died, his scent so strong it had sent her into a faint. Now, she found it comforting. That and knowing he was near. He still existed in some form.

Maybe if she was very good at whatever he needed her to do, she could keep helping him. Then she could see him all the time. Now that was something she could look forward to.

~~*~~

Jessica floated into her little cottage on the water. It was the same one she'd had in Maine, but nicer because she had no bills to pay, no chores to attend to, and no traffic to deal with. That's what she loved about the afterlife. It was all the best of being alive. She still looked the same, thought the same, even breathed and had a heartbeat, at least that's how it felt, but she had none of the irritations. She couldn't even get sick.

Then again, she now had a rather large irritation in the form of Duncan Montgomerie. Usually, after her Spirit Guide training sessions, she enjoyed sitting on the front porch watching the water lap at the rocky shoreline, the temperatures a perfect summer day, but right now all she wanted was her couch and a bowl of ice cream.

She stalked into her bedroom, phased to solid, and changed into a pair of jean shorts and a tank top, then hung her suit on the door. That Cameron Douglas had refused her request for a new mentor had rankled. He was so confident in Duncan's abilities, that talking to Cameron was like talking to a wall of granite. He acted like he had little time for her but there was no such thing as time in the afterlife.

There was no way she would ask Duncan for more information on Holly. He just plain pissed her off. She was determined to ace this case, despite Mr. Distraction's know-it-all attitude. She needed to learn as much as she could, more than Duncan anyway, to do that.

After a long walk along the coast, she'd finally gathered her courage and bopped into the cute little house next to the Christmas shop on the main street of Deervale. She'd witnessed Holly meeting Cameron's spirit for the first time. It was so heartbreaking she couldn't stay. Holly's fall into her beautiful Christmas tree and then the look in Cameron's eyes when his wife started to cry had just been too much. Besides, it was a private moment that she had no right to witness.

Pushing her glasses farther up the bridge of her nose, she walked to the refrigerator and pulled out her favorite ice cream from the freezer, pistachio. Forgoing a bowl, she grabbed a spoon then snuggled into the corner of her couch with the carton.

From what she could tell, there was no such thing as calories in the afterlife. Thankful she'd finally mastered the art of solidifying and phasing at will so she could enjoy her earthly pleasure, she took a bite of the sweet, cold dessert. As the nutty flavor washed over her tongue, she closed her eyes in sheer bliss. Now *this* was heaven. Opening her eyes to take another bite, she froze. "What are you doing here?"

Duncan floated on the arm at the other end of her couch, looking absolutely delicious in his jeans, t-shirt and socks. Socks?

"This is when your private lessons start." The sexy grin he gave her had her swallowing hard as excitement skittered across her skin and into her groin.

Shit. The man was a walking tease. Make that a floating tease.

She wanted Mr. Knows-It-All back. He was easier to deal with. Not sure what to say, she dipped her spoon in the carton and took another bite as her mind raced. What kind of lessons? From his look, her bedroom would be the proper place for them.

"What are you eating?" He leaned forward and squinted at the carton.

She swallowed and tried for a professional air. "Pistachio ice cream."

"I dinna think I've ever tried that flavor." His body phased to solid and he plucked the carton from her hand.

"Hey! The least you can do is ask."

He shrugged as he dipped his finger into the green ice cream. "You'd just tell me I could have some, so why bother?" He lifted his finger and stuck the ice cream in his mouth. "Hmmm, this *is* good. No wonder it's your favorite." His grin could have talked a Sunday school teacher into stripping.

She stared, her body revving at the sight of him dipping his finger in again while her brain caught up to his words. "How do you know it's my favorite?"

He winked. "I know everything about you."

She flushed as her body heated. Crap, this man was a flirt if she'd ever seen one and his lilting accent didn't help. She reached across the couch and grabbed the ice cream out of his hand. "If you don't mind, I was enjoying that."

He chuckled. "Oh, touchy."

Why did she now feel like a bitch? She wasn't like this usually. Mr. Distraction had her off balance and she didn't like it.

If only Cameron could have given her a different mentor. Duncan Montgomerie would ruin her concentration and make fun of any mistake she might make. Her definition of "mentor" was not that. "I'm assuming you came here for a reason? I mean, besides the beautiful view." She pointed toward the windows with her spoon.

He glanced that way before letting his gaze roam from the tops of her bare feet, over her legs, past her shorts to the stretchy fabric of her white tank-covered chest. She held her breath, waiting for his eyes to meet hers, but they stayed riveted on her breasts. Thankful she'd left her bra on so he couldn't see how hard her nipples had turned at his perusal, she moved the ice cream to block his view and took another bite to cool down.

He smirked at her move. "As I said, it's time for your private lessons. I thought you'd be more comfortable here than at my castle."

She stilled at his comment. "You live in a castle?"

"Of course. It's where I lived before my death. That is one of the elements of the afterlife that you need to know. How we look, where we live. Our knowledge is frozen in the state we were in when we died."

That made sense to her. "Do you know how I died? I can't recall."

He shook his head. "No and you won't. I dinna know how I died either. That is the one change in our appearance. There is no evidence of how our lives ended. Or memory either. For all I know, I was shot in the heart in a duel."

A duel? "Is that a possibility? Were you caught sleeping with some man's wife?"

Duncan burst into laughter. "No, I never slept with a married lady, but a father or older brother of some lovely who pretended to be pure to her family could very well have cried foul." He shrugged. "Doesn't really matter now, does it?"

Jessica frowned. Her curiosity about her own death was a little stronger than Duncan's. She didn't even remember what she'd been doing when she died. She hadn't been in poor health so it must have been an accident or something. At age thirty-three, she thought of herself as in her prime.

She looked down at the ice cream melting in the cartoon and

scooped out one more spoonful before she rose and walked to the freezer to put it away. She sent a mental request for another two pints of Pistachio and a carton of Cherry Vanilla. Then she dropped the spoon in the sink, well aware it would be clean and in the drawer when she went to use it again. The afterlife was pretty sweet. Her wishes were granted as she requested them. She just wished she'd lived her life to the fullest first. She'd even put off her own wedding for two years. What woman did that?

"You're still frowning, lass."

She spun at the sound of Duncan's voice in her right ear. He'd stood right behind her. She pressed her back against the counter to add a couple inches between them.

He grasped the counter on either side of her, his Christmassy scent filling her nose. It was so strong when he wasn't phased.

"I like you solid. I can smell…" He inhaled, his large chest expanding, filling the airspace between them and brushing against her breasts. "Cranberry."

"You can't smell that." He couldn't, could he? It was the local soap she used, handmade by an older woman in the small town she had lived in.

He looked down at her, his lips slightly curved as usual. "Aye, I can, lass. And it smells tart yet sweet. Edible."

She pushed against his chest to step away, but he didn't budge. "Do you mind?"

His grin grew. "Actually, I do. There's something we need to discuss before we start your assignment."

She arched her brow. "Really? And we have to do it right here in my kitchen?"

He lowered his head, bringing his light beard closer, his lips closer. "Aye, because it has to do with the blush in your cheeks, the heat radiating from your body, and the shorter breaths ye be taking that push your delectable breasts into my chest."

Her heart went into double time at his heavier accented words while her brain ceased to function as her gaze riveted on his mouth. He would kiss her. Her body primed for contact and her mouth opened, ready.

Guilt niggled at the back of her brain when his lips brushed against hers. Even as her body strained toward him, her mind told her this was wrong. Reacting to that signal, she phased. His arms, as she passed through, caused tiny tingles to erupt across her breasts.

He turned to face her. "You dinna play fair, Jessica."

She took a deep breath to gather her thoughts. "I'm not playing at all. But you are. Why the full come-on all of a sudden? When I saw you last, you were treating me like a little girl who needed her hand held."

His smile faltered. "I realized my mistake when I saw you in those revealing clothes. You are obviously very much a woman."

"No kidding. And this *woman* is engaged. I mean, I was, I mean…" She shut her mouth at how stupid she must sound. It was such a habit to be faithful to her fiancé.

Being dead was new for her. One of her biggest regrets was not having married Jacob. She'd finally started planning the wedding after being engaged for two years. Her stomach knotted. It was her fault they never became man and wife.

Duncan smiled sympathetically, for once not in amusement. "I know you were."

She could handle Duncan "the flirt," but this "real" Duncan was too much. "I still consider myself engaged, so you'll have to excuse me if I can't shut my feelings off so quickly." She floated back to the living room to stare out the window, letting the rhythm of the water calm her frazzled nerves.

She'd been in the afterlife awhile, though how long she couldn't be sure. It seemed like a few years. She should have come to terms with it by now, but obviously she hadn't, at least not completely.

Duncan made himself at home on her couch, distracting her as his solid persona reflected in the window. It seemed rude to stay phased, so she solidified again and turned to face him. Maybe she should focus on their case instead of herself. She was good at that. "Should we talk about Holly?"

He cocked his head. "Holly?"

"Yes, Holly." At his blank expression, she shook her head as she looked toward the ceiling, searching for the patience she usually used with clients. "Holly Douglas, our supervisor's wife?"

"Oh, *that* Holly. She is no' my wife, so I have no reason to keep track of her first name. She's Mrs. Douglas to me."

"Fine. Should we talk about Mrs. Douglas?" She moved to a comfortable chair with an ottoman she had positioned directly across from the couch. "What strategy are we going to use? Are the times in her life we visit predetermined or do we get to choose? I had some thoughts on that as I think picking the rights ones—"

"Stop. You're making my head spin." Duncan's smile had turned into a grimace. "I've already chosen the times in Mrs. Douglas' life that we will visit with her, after receiving Cameron's guidance."

"What? When did you do that? Why wasn't I involved? Isn't this my case?"

Duncan's eyes widened, his surprise at her outburst causing her blood to boil all the more.

"I'm your mentor so it was my responsibility. When you are experienced enough to work alone, then you will confer with Cameron."

She glared at him. "I'm not a newbie. I know what to do."

Duncan's smile was so condescending, she stood before he could say anything else. "Fine. Then let's get started."

"Hold on, lass. You can't go in those short pants and revealing top."

Jessica flushed. He must think her a complete idiot since she *had* forgotten what she wore. She knew this wouldn't go well with him as her mentor. "I didn't mean this second. I planned to change. Just wait here." She stalked off, ignoring his knowing smile.

Once in her bedroom, she whipped off her tank and shorts and threw them on the bed. She opened the closet door, barely keeping it from banging against the wall. The man was an ass. No, he was an arrogant ass. He thought all he had to do was smile and she'd jump into bed with him. She wasn't that stupid.

She scanned her clothes, looking for something to wear. She'd planned on a skirt suit to look professional, but having seen the heartache in Holly's eyes, she preferred to appear friendly. Her gaze landed on a button-down sky-blue blouse. Perfect. She could wear that with the matching long crinkle skirt. A wide white spandex belt at her waist would complete the look. It was sort of angelic and yet not.

Despite her anger at Duncan, she found herself more relaxed and excited at the prospect of helping Holly. Throwing the clothing on the bed, she closed the closet door only to find Duncan floating behind it. "Ack!"

Crossing her hand over her chest, she tried to slow her heart at his scare. "What part of 'wait here' didn't you understand?"

His grin froze on his face as he took in her white push-up bra and boy shorts panties.

At the man's speechless stare, a sudden confidence filled her. It was good to know she could affect him as much as he affected her. She raised her arms to the sides. "Now you've seen what you can't have." She stepped forward and waved her hands through him. "Get out of here so I can get dressed."

He shivered as her hands broke into his phased state.

Did he feel the tingles too? Was that normal for everyone or just them? She didn't plan to ask.

Duncan didn't respond except to float back through the wall. Served him right, sneaking into her room while she was changing.

She donned her clothing and strode into the living room where she found her mentor back on the couch, studying one of her seashells. She didn't want to admit it, but the connection between them had her feeling a bit unsettled. "Okay, I'm ready."

Duncan's quick smile was back in place. "You do know in your phased form you can just think what you'd like to wear and it will be on you."

"Really?"

He quirked his brow, once more looking like he was instructing a child. "Aye, I taught you that in my training. Do you also remember we cannot, for any reason, become solid among the living?"

She nodded, though she'd missed that part too. Damn, what else did she miss that was critically important from his training? "I just don't remember why."

Duncan's eyes widened. "If we turn solid among the living, we will immediately cease to exist."

Oh crap, she really wished she'd paid more attention in his class. If she'd only known what a jerk he could be, she would have.

His smile returned. "You look lovely, lass. I think Holly will be very happy to have you as her Spirit of Christmas Past."

She looked for any sign of teasing, but found none. Now why did he have to go and be nice, just when she'd placed him in the "jerk" category?

"Ready?" He looked at her expectantly.

Immediately, she phased. "Ready."

He gave her an approving smile then phased himself and they both floated down to the living room of Holly Douglas.

Duncan watched, fascinated, as Jessica's face softened when she gazed at Holly asleep in her husband's chair. The flickering Christmas lights reflected off Jessica's light, silky hair, making it look almost alive and very inviting. Now if she would just leave it loose.

She looked at him. "Do we wake her?" She whispered her question so softly he almost didn't hear it, but since his gaze had dropped to her lips, he may have actually figured it out by her lip movement.

He leaned in to whisper in her ear, her cranberry scent still heady even though it was lighter in her phased state. He loved that smell. It reminded him of Christmas with his parents and brother. Cranberries were a rare treat, just like Jessica. "No' until the clock strikes eleven."

A shiver ran through her, but she didn't look at him, just nodded.

When he'd entered her room to tell her about dressing while phasing, he hadn't expected to find her undressed. Her body was everything he liked in a woman. Breasts that would fit a man's hands well, hips big enough to hold on to while thrusting, and thighs that would make a comfortable pillow before tasting what they hid. All that womanly pleasure hidden beneath her clothing had caused him to harden, even in a phased state. Luckily, he'd exited before she noticed.

He didn't understand her. Then again, he hadn't mentored a woman in a long while. He hadn't even noticed that oddity until Cameron had assigned her to him. He'd swear he'd had at least a hundred mentees since his last woman. There was definitely a message in that. Maybe Cameron had waited for a female mentee who wouldn't fall to his charms. Jessica certainly hadn't if *Now you've seen what you can't have*, was any indication. That definitely rankled. He would need to find another approach to working with her, one he wasn't as confident in.

Jessica grabbed his wrist and pointed with her other hand. The woman's cat had woken. It stared at them as if it had been expecting them. Then it yawned and laid its head down on its paw and went back to sleep.

She let go of his arm and pushed her glasses up the bridge of her nose. Her excitement was almost palpable and it had him looking at their mission in a different light. Had he ever been that eager to be a Spirit Guide? They were only the first spirits to visit Mrs. Douglas. Holly. On one hand, that meant they didn't have the biggest responsibility, but on the other hand, they could set the tone for her transformation, making the odds for success much higher. His gut told him that's exactly what Jessica would want.

The clock started to bong and he grasped Jessica's hand to hold her back. She gave him a frustrated look, but he held up his other hand. Since they were both phased, they could feel each other and her pulse was racing. He wanted it to race beneath him, but getting her into his bed would take some time.

As the last bong sounded, Holly woke and looked around in confusion.

He let go of Jessica's hand and nodded. Usually, he approached the living when with a new Spirit Guide, but she was so anxious to help, he didn't want to risk an argument in front of Holly.

Jessica floated to a stop next to the cat. "Hi, Holly. I'm Jessica. Cameron sent me. I'm the Spirit of Christmas Past."

Holly blinked and rubbed her eyes. "He said you'd come."

Knock him off his feet and drop him in the bog, he'd never seen an introduction go that easily. Usually the living would scream, cry, even run at the sight of a Spirit Guide. One of these two women was extraordinary. Either that or it was easier for Holly because Cameron was her husband and someone she already trusted. That kind of trust was rare.

Jessica knelt down next to Holly's chair. "Merry Christmas Eve."

Holly pulled the lounging chair to an upright position and stared at Jessica. "You look familiar. Did we ever meet?"

"I don't know. You don't look familiar to me. Maybe Cameron chose me because he knew you would feel comfortable with me."

Holly nodded, but continued to stare.

"We're going to show you some of the happy times of your life. I think it will be fun." Jessica smiled so kindly that Duncan suddenly wanted her to smile at him like that, too.

He shook his head. The chances of that were about as high as a woman winning a golf game…during his lifetime. So much had changed with the living, it was hard to keep up.

Holly interrupted his thoughts. "We? Oh yes, Cam said something about you bringing a man with you."

Jessica pointed to him. "He's a friend of mine. This is Duncan Montgomerie."

His heart warmed at Jessica's reference to him as a friend and he floated a little closer. "Hello, lass. It's a pleasure to make your acquaintance. I knew your husband had good taste, but he outdid himself when he found you."

Holly looked from him to Jessica. "Player?"

Jessica nodded and the women shared a smile.

He wasn't sure what he missed. He did play golf, but Jessica didn't know that. While he had a whole file on her, she didn't know anything about him. Probably some women's intuition thing or of that ilk.

Holly looked back at him. "It's nice to meet you, too." Then she stood, folding the wool blanket she had covered herself with and placing it across the back of the recliner. "Do I need to get my coat?"

Jessica stood as well. "No. The temperatures won't affect us and those sweatpants look very comfortable."

"Oh, they are. So is this sweater. I got it at—oh, I'm sorry. I'm not used to talking to ghosts. Honestly, Cam was the first one I ever met." She looked away.

Duncan noticed the shift in Holly's countenance as soon as she mentioned Cameron. Her sadness was deep. It would be a lot of work to ease it.

Jessica noticed it too and floated into Holly's line of sight. "It's no problem. Actually, I'm not a ghost. A ghost is an entity with unfinished business among the living which keeps it here. I'm a spirit and I exist on another plane."

Holly's curiosity was evident.

Jessica *was* good. She'd distracted Holly with a little information, not that she should have shared it, but this was a special case since Holly was Cameron's wife.

"So does that mean Cam is a spirit too?"

"Yes." Jessica placed her hand on Holly's arm. "But tonight is about you, not us. That's what we want to focus on, okay?"

Holly nodded but didn't look Jessica in the eyes.

Hmm, that was interesting.

Jessica turned toward him. "Are you ready?" She looked back at Holly. "Duncan has the itinerary."

"Aye, and we're going to a stop in your childhood first." He kept his smile compassionate.

Jessica nodded. "That sounds like fun. Now, you'll feel a little coolness as I phase you so you can't be seen."

"Oh. That *is* strange." Holly looked at her hands. "I can see the rug right through my hands." She turned them over and back. "This is how Cameron was when he visited me. I really wanted to hold him." Her eyes began to water.

"I know." Jessica took Holly's hand. "That's one of those lines that can't be crossed. But we don't need to think about that. What we should be setting our sights on is exploring the happiness you have had."

Holly sniffed and nodded.

"Aw, Holly." Jessica enfolded the woman in a hug and Holly wrapped her arms around Jessica tight. "I know it hurts."

Blow him over with an 18 pounder cannon. He hadn't expected that. He'd never had a living person connect so with his other trainees.

Cameron must know his wife well and chose a female Spirit Guide who she could relate to. After all, they were both from America. This could make their assignment that much easier.

The differences between the two ladies was striking as they hugged. Jessica was tall, blonde and curvy. While Holly had a similar shape, she was much shorter and dark haired. In his past, he'd always been interested in darker-haired women, but Jessica was not only pretty, in her controlled fashion, she had a personality that intrigued him. This assignment would definitely be an enjoyable one.

When the two women split apart, Jessica continued to hold Holly's hand. "Are you ready now for some fun?"

Holly nodded and wiped her eyes with the back of her other hand. A small smile formed on her lips and it was clear, she already trusted Jessica to make her feel better. A niggling doubt about this sudden connection wormed its way into Duncan's mind.

"Duncan?" Jessica looked at him expectantly.

He took Holly's other hand. "Ladies." Without another word, he floated them out through the roof.

Chapter Three

"Oh wow, this is amazing. It's like hang gliding but slower." Holly's eyes were wide with excitement.

Below them the small town of Deervale was asleep and the mechanical Christmas lights on houses tinged the streets pink. He guided them over Scotland toward the ocean. "Did you wish to go faster, lass?"

"No." Jessica frowned at him. "This is fine."

He grinned even as he shook his head. "Spoilsport."

Holly's chuckle had him thinking. Maybe banter between himself and Jessica could help.

Just as they reached the coast, the scenery went black as he sped them back through time.

Holly clasped his hand tighter.

He gave her a reassuring squeeze. "No need to fret. We're almost there."

He'd no sooner spoke the words than the tall evergreens of New Hampshire came into view, but the dark night was broken by flashing red lights illuminating great billows of smoke and the snow-packed ground.

Slowly, they descended.

Holly gasped. "Oh. This was the Christmas fire from when I was ten. We lost everything."

Jessica scowled at him over Holly's head. He was confused as well, but Cameron had insisted on this time on this particular Christmas Eve, so he cocked his head toward the fire, silently entreating her to watch.

"There I am." Holly pulled from their grasp and floated to where a woman holding a young girl's hand stood talking to a fireman.

He and Jessica followed.

"No." Jessica's word stopped him and he turned to find her floating in one place, staring at the little girl. "It can't be."

Even in the flickering light of fire trucks and flames, even though she was phased, he could see her face had paled considerably. He floated back to her, concerned. "What is it?"

"I know this place."

He nodded. "Aye, that would make sense since you also lived in this state for a time."

"No." She shook her head. "I mean I know this fire. I was here."

She was absolutely sure so he didn't argue, but he'd never been with a mentee who had been sent back to an event in their own life before. Then again, maybe that was why Cameron chose Jessica for Holly. Everything about this assignment was different than the norm. It would be best not to make her aware of that. It was her first case and she needed to feel comfortable. "If you and Holly connected in the past then that will help her trust you. This is good."

She moved her gaze from the little girl and looked at him, her eyes watering. "I don't understand how this can be a happy occurrence for her. I was able to help them for the night, but then they were on their own. I always regretted not having the time to follow up. She must hate me."

He had the urge to comfort her, which was completely foreign to him. He usually stayed very far away from tears. "I can't believe anyone would hate you. I doubt Cameron would have sent you for Holly if she hated you."

She sniffed and pushed her glasses up before nodding. "You're right. Let's see what's happening."

They floated over just as a young Jessica stepped into the lights. Duncan's heart skipped a beat. Not only was her full beauty just beginning to show, but her compassion was breathtaking. Uncomfortable with his feelings, he grinned. "Wow, you were beautiful back then."

"And I'm not now? Thanks." She gave him an exasperated look and returned her focus to the scene unfolding before them.

Holly chuckled again and he bumped his elbow into Jessica. Instead of appreciating his joke, she ignored him. Bollocks. The woman needed to "chill," as he'd heard recent American recruits say.

"I knew I recognized you." Holly, who floated in front of them, turned to address Jessica.

She stiffened beside him as if she expected someone to attack her.

"You're the one who introduced us to Grandma and Grandpa Tinder."

Jessica's eyes widened. "You mean the Foster Grandparents I asked to house you for the night?"

Holly's face lit with a wide smile. "Yes. I can't wait to see them again as they were. I was so skeptical back then. Everything had gone wrong since Mom and I moved into that low-income apartment building, thanks to the help of some social worker. That soured me on anyone who wanted to give us a hand. I figured the Tinders were in it for money or to feel better than others. I was so wrong."

As Holly turned her attention back to the scene unfolding before them, Duncan whispered in Jessica's ear, "I told you."

She swatted him away and he chuckled. He had another goal for this assignment now. To get Jessica to relax more and enjoy her afterlife. Why did he care about that?

He lost his smile as he tried to figure it out and when he did, he grinned at her, though she wasn't looking at him. If Jessica learned to "loosen up" then the chances of them enjoying a bed were much, much higher. He didn't care which bed. Sometimes he was quite impressed with his own instincts.

"Jessica, look." Holly pointed to two older people exiting a tan sedan. Grandpa helped his wife across the trampled snow. He was a tall man in brown corduroys and a plaid wool jacket. His short hair was liberally sprinkled with white. His wife was pudgy with frosted hair and a warm smile. Her big parka fell to her thighs and she wore jeans. What was it with Americans and jeans? Duncan pulled at his neckline, feeling suffocated again.

Holly glanced back for a second. "Grandpa Tinder always said Grandma was his most precious possession."

"I can see that." Jessica's voice was kind, but the minute Holly turned back, Jessica's smile disappeared.

What was she afraid of?

"Hey, wait a minute." Holly spun around to face them. "You don't look much older than me now, but you had to be at least ten years older than me back then."

Jessica's face paled.

Blast, he hadn't expected anything like this. "She looks young because things are different when you are a Spirit."

"Oh, that makes sense." Holly turned back to watch the interaction between the Tinders, young Jessica, and herself and her mom.

Duncan pulled Jessica aside to converse privately. "What's wrong?"

"What isn't? I thought I'd only been in training a few years." She looked devastated.

He laid his hand on her shoulder. "The Spirit Guide training is very long. I dinna ke—know what it is in the time of the living because it's irrelevant. Time doesn't matter anymore."

Jessica nodded, but was clearly not convinced. "Did it take me longer to complete it than most recruits?"

He smiled as understanding dawned. "Actually, you were one of the quickest to finish in my entire memory of training Spirit Guides."

"Really?" Her wish to be the best was endearing and not unlike a number of male trainees he'd had, but he sensed the need for success stemmed from a different place with Jessica. From her need to help others. From her heart.

"Aye." He squeezed her shoulder then forced himself to let go. "But you were nervous even before Holly brought up your age difference. What are you afraid of?"

"What?" She looked away. "No, I'm just trying to figure out why this event is considered a happy one for Holly. If I remember correctly, she and her mom lost everything."

She wasn't telling him the entire truth. Something else bothered her. But she made a good point. He had a feeling it had to do with her brief moment in Holly's life, but he wouldn't tell her that. "I'm sure Cameron knows what he's doing. It *is* his wife and he wants her happy."

"Of course, you're right. We should get back there."

"Jessica?"

She halted after floating a foot or so. "Yes."

He'd been about to tell her no' to get too wrapped up in the visit to Holly's past, but his gut said it would fall on deaf ears and it would make him sound like he cared far more than he did. "Your choice of clothing was perfect for this." He let his grin widen as relief and confidence filled her face. "And ye look good enough to eat."

She rolled her eyes and sped back to Holly.

He laughed loudly, sure she heard him when Holly glanced back. He winked at her and she smiled.

Holly glanced at Jessica before turning back to watch her history unfold.

He drifted toward them, enjoying himself far more than he'd first expected. The Tinders, along with young Holly and her mom, were just entering one of the moving conveyances that were everywhere in the current time period when he joined Jessica and Holly.

"Can we follow them to their house?" Holly addressed him directly.

"Of course." He glanced at Jessica. "Is that acceptable to you?"

She bestowed a fake smile on Holly as she nodded, but Holly was too excited to notice. He noticed though. "Take my hands, ladies." This time he purposefully put himself between the women, a chance to touch Jessica could no' be passed up. Jessica's light cranberry scent mingled with Holly's, who smelled like apples to him. The combination reminded him of the kitchens at Rossan and caused him to grin. No wonder journeys into the past could make people happy.

As he sped them to the Tinders' house, he squeezed Jessica's hand. She glanced at him, her expression filled with worry, and he gave her what he hoped was a reassuring smile. There was something she hadn't told him about this night. He needed to get her away and discover what it was.

As they arrived, everyone had just finished dinner. He purposefully timed it so Holly could see what happened once she went to bed. Cameron had told him about this episode.

Holly inhaled deeply. "Can you smell that lasagna? Grandma Tinder had made a big batch to bring to her daughter's house, but they cancelled their plans when they got the call that we needed help. I should have felt bad, but that night I was too selfish and was thankful I got to eat the food instead. Talk about comfort food."

Jessica placed her hand on Holly's shoulder. "I'm sure the

family understood. You had just lost everything. Sacrificing a meal for you was just a little something they were happy to do."

"Oh, but they did so much more. Look."

Grandma Tinder got up and moved to the counter and addressed Holly's mom. "Ms. Thomas told us you also had a thousand dollars saved in a cookie jar. Jim and I do the same thing and never thought about how it would feel if our house burned down. So we discussed it while you were getting changed, and well…" She reached behind her and lifted a ceramic cookie jar shaped like a black bear. "We want you to have ours."

Holly's mother shook her head and argued that it wasn't right, she couldn't take their money and that they had done so much already, but the Tinders insisted. Finally, her mother took the jar.

Jim sat at the head of the table, his arms crossed and smiling from ear to ear. "Go ahead, open it."

Holly spoke over her shoulder. "Watch this."

Duncan grinned at her excitement before glancing at Jessica to see she waited with bated breath.

Holly's mom opened the jar and reached her hand in to pull out a wad of hundred dollar bills. "Oh, I can't take this."

Jim beamed from where he sat. "Too late. You already accepted the gift. You can't give it back now. It would make us look bad."

Holly spun around, even as her younger self got up and ran to hug her mom. "There was almost five thousand dollars in that jar. To say we were thankful would be an understatement." She gave Jessica an unexpected hug. "Thank you so much for finding the Tinders for us."

After a shocked second, Jessica hugged Holly back. Duncan liked the warmth in his chest at the emotional display. Maybe after this success, Jessica would relax a bit.

When Holly finally let go, there were tears in Jessica's eyes. "I'm so glad I could help."

Holly looked at him. "After that we just went to bed."

"That's true, lass, but I'm thinking you might want to see what happened next."

"Really? Isn't that a bit like spying?"

He shrugged. "Aye."

Holly's eyes gleamed with mischief. "Okay, I'm game."

The three of them watched as the young Holly went upstairs with her mother. As soon as they disappeared from sight, Grandma sat down next to Grandpa. "I really like them."

"Me too."

Grandma pulled on Jim's crossed arms. "No, I mean I really like them."

He let her grasp his hand. "You've got that Christmas gleam in your eye, sweetie. I can practically see your mind working a mile a minute. Tell me what you're thinking."

"I'm thinking Holly is about the same age as Melanie and her mom is about the same size as Valerie."

Jim cocked an eyebrow. "You want to give these girls your daughter and granddaughter's Christmas gifts?"

Grandma Tinder nodded, her lips pursed together as if she couldn't contain her wonderful idea, and she couldn't. "Can you just see the looks on these girls faces when they find presents under our tree just for them. What do you say?"

Jim kissed his wife's hand. "I say I have the most giving woman in the world for my wife. Let's do it."

"That's my man." Grandma got up and hugged her husband. "I'll need some help changing the tags and getting everything under the tree."

Grandpa stood and took his wife into his arms. "Have I told you I loved you today?"

Grandma thought for a moment and nodded. "Yup, just after I made you your poached eggs for breakfast, but you know I never tire of hearing it."

He kissed her on the lips and let go. "Nope. Once a day is enough. I don't want to spoil you."

As Jim walked toward a back hallway, Grandma went after him. "You are such a tease, Mr. Tinder."

"And you are such a perfect one to tease, Mrs. Tinder."

The room was empty but none of them moved. Duncan's throat had tightened at the generosity and love in the house. For the first time in his afterlife, a tiny regret burrowed into his heart, but to acknowledge it would be to give it strength.

Holly floated to the table where the two older people had sat. Jessica swallowed hard and glanced at him. Her eyes revealed she was more affected by what they'd seen than Holly.

"I didn't know." Holly raised her hands out to the side. "All this. I had almost believed in Santa Claus again the next morning when there were presents for me under the tree. Mom was convinced they'd found a twenty-four-hour department store and snuck out while we were sleeping." She smiled. "I'm so glad we had that fire."

Jessica floated toward Holly. "I had no idea."

Holly continued, like she felt a need to tell them. "They even skipped going to Christmas dinner at their oldest son's house because they didn't want to leave us. So they made two chickens they had in the freezer and we had the best Christmas ever."

"I never knew that." Jessica looked at Holly as if she were an angel herself. "Your case was so different from everyone else at that apartment complex. Half the people had family and the other half qualified for government programs, but you and your mom had neither. The only choice I had was a homeless shelter and I just couldn't do that to you on Christmas."

Holly grinned. "And Cameron says *I* have the biggest heart." She winked at Duncan.

Jessica shook her head. "It was Christmas. Anyone would have done the same."

Holly widened her eyes at Duncan. He agreed with her, but it was obvious Jessica didn't see the beauty of her own heart. "So where did the Tinders come from?"

"I was so desperate to find Holly an alternative place to sleep that night, I asked a coworker if she had any volunteers who might be willing to help. She oversaw the Foster Grandparent program which actually connects older adults with children, but I was desperate." Jessica looked from him to Holly. "My coworker went on maternity leave that Christmas and when she got back, I'd forgotten to ask her how you fared."

Duncan loved the way her eyes shined with joy. She sincerely loved helping others and it had him looking at his own motivations.

Holly rested her hand on Jessica's shoulder. "I'm so glad you did because Grandma and Grandpa let us use their summer cottage on a pond in Canterbury for free and told us it was a trial period. If we liked it enough, they would insulate it and then we could pay rent. Of course, we loved it and it was closer to mom's work."

"They did that, too?" Jessica looked stunned.

Holly nodded. "We still call them Grandma and Grandpa. Their whole family adopted us until mom married John, their third eldest son. Then we really were family."

Duncan smiled at the happiness he felt radiating from Holly as she watched Mr. and Mrs. Tinder walk through the room with arms full of presents. As they headed into the living room, Holly floated after them.

He glanced at Jessica, who appeared a bit stunned but happy as well. What other surprises did Cameron have in store for them? His own excitement about the assignment ramped up.

He grasped Jessica's hand and phased them back to her place.

Jessica pulled away and stared at Duncan in horror. "What happened? Why are we here? We can't leave Holly there alone. We need to go back, right now."

He grabbed her hand again but she tried to twist away.

Duncan pulled her into his arms. "Shhh, lass it's okay. She is no' alone. We're with her."

She stopped squirming. "What do you mean?"

"I mean, there's no time in the afterlife. No time is passing for us. When we return, it will be the same time as when we left."

She tried to wrap her mind around that. It did make sense, but it was still hard to truly understand. Maybe when they got back, it would help her see. In the meantime, she was held against the very hard chest of her mentor and after the surprise she'd just had, she wasn't in a hurry to back away. "I think I understand. But why did you bring us back?"

He loosened his arms a bit and met her gaze. "Because you just had a shock and I wanted you to have time to understand it."

She stiffened. "I grasped what just happened. I'm not stupid."

She felt him take a deep breath. "That's no' what I meant. I think the term you would use is…is…" His brow furrowed as he thought, then his smile returned. "Process it. You need time to process it."

It was too thoughtful of him for her heart not to notice. Who was Mr. Duncan Montgomerie really and how could she find out?

He pulled her tighter against him and kissed her hair. Then he let her go.

She wanted to stay in his arms, which made no sense. The man was a seducer. He was only interested in one thing, wasn't he? She still took the opportunity to put some space between them as she "processed" what he'd just done for her.

"Did you see the joy on her face?" He solidified before plopping onto the couch, his large body taking up half the space with his arms spread across the top and his legs crossed in front of him.

The warmth she'd felt at Holly's happiness spread throughout her body again, even as she solidified too. It was so exciting. "Yes.

The sorrow that hangs around her all the time was squashed for a moment. Do you think we have a chance? Because to be honest, I had my doubts at the start of this."

He grinned up at her, his own thrill lighting his eyes with a deep-blue light. "I do. But we've only just begun. She's too young to have so much sadness. It will be difficult to bring her to a level the next spirit can work with, but we've made a great start."

She nodded then moved to the chair across from him. She sat and bent her knees, lifting her feet to the chair and hugging her legs. "I agree. I guess Cameron knew what he was doing when he sent us to that fire."

"Aye, I never doubted it. He's the best supervisor I've had and I've had many."

"How long have you been training Spirit Guides?" She couldn't contain her curiosity, though she'd promised herself she would.

He shrugged. "I dinna know. Can't even remember how many supervisors."

"Will it be like that for me too? Always being a Spirit Guide?"

"That's up to you." He hesitated, as if he chose his words carefully. "Some switch duties."

Yes, she remembered looking at a list, but as soon as she'd read the job description for Spirit Guide, she'd made her choice.

"And some…they move on."

"Move on?" What was there to move on to? "Where do they go?"

He uncrossed his legs. "I am no' entirely sure. It's been whispered they achieve paradise, but I doubt that. I've been here probably a couple hundred living years, so if that were the case, why haven't I moved on?"

She tried to wrap her brain around this new information. So there *was* some sort of hierarchy here, or maybe those who moved on went to an area of the afterlife Duncan didn't know about. He didn't appear to be incredibly inquisitive. "Personally, I think this is paradise. I have my comfortable house, a profession I love and my same youthful body."

At the mention of her body, Duncan leaned forward, his forearms on his spread knees. "I was only jesting about how gorgeous you were when you were younger. That was just the tip of the iceberg compared to now. I just said it to get Holly to smile."

She pushed her glasses up, flushing at his compliment. "I know. I caught on afterward. I shouldn't have scowled at you either when we first arrived at the fire. I was just so taken aback by arriving at such a scene. Even once I recognized it, I couldn't imagine how it could be a happy memory. I have to have faith in you and Cameron."

Duncan reached his hand toward her. "Truce."

She dropped her legs and shook his hand just before he pulled her on top of him. "Duncan!" His hard body beneath hers felt like solid muscle and every soft spot on hers liked it.

"Aye?"

"I thought we were having a truce. Let me up."

"We have to kiss on it first."

"What?" She tried to leverage herself off his chest but his arms were like steel bands around her.

"Shaking hands is what your time period does. In my time, we kissed."

She stilled for a moment and stared at him. "You kissed men?"

He threw his head back and laughed.

She'd never met a person who was happy so much of the time.

"Ach, lass, you're goin' to make me split me pants."

At the mention of his pants, she became keenly aware that his crotch rested beneath her abdomen.

He grinned at her. "I dinna kiss men, but with women we seal our agreements with a kiss, no' a shaking of hands."

She opened her mouth to argue the point, but his lips came up to hers, catching her off guard.

His tongue didn't hesitate to breach her lips and his strong arms held her in place as he explored her mouth, filling her nostrils with his pine scent and curling her toes with his mastery over the kiss. His tongue explored her, tangling with her own even as the hand that held her head tilted it a bit more so he could thoroughly taste her.

Spikes of desire swirled through her body like a water spout, sending pleasure in all directions. She'd lost total thought process when he stopped and stared at her, a strange look on his face, as if he'd just kissed a ghost. Bemused, she gave him a soft smile. Technically, she was a kind of ghost but then again so was he.

She could feel his rapid heartbeat beneath her breast just before his muscles tensed and he pulled her up and sat her back in her chair before he strode to her bay window.

Really? They share an amazing kiss and then he gets up and walks away?

Duncan stood staring at the ocean. Was the kiss really just a way to seal their truce? It could very well be. She was silly for expecting it to be anything more with a man like him. Too bad she couldn't look at sex like he did. Still, she couldn't help touching her lips since his back was turned.

He spoke toward the window. "Are you pleased to learn Holly had a wonderful childhood with the Tinders' help?"

Holly? Oh right, the case. How could she have let him distract her? That's right, he was Mr. Distraction and very good at it. "Of course I am. I'm just surprised. I felt like I hadn't completed my job. I always regretted not finding out what had happened to Holly and her mom. It was the only fire I worked on a Christmas Eve. It felt so wrong for them to lose everything that night."

"Were you always thorough?" He continued to talk to the ocean.

"I tried to be. But being a social worker in America was very busy. I rarely had time to sleep, never mind have a life." She sighed. "There were so many clients. We were supposed to handle a case load of forty, but mine rose to sixty a number of times. There was so much need."

Duncan turned. "And they all needed you?"

"Not me in particular." She rose—the remembered stress of her job made her want to move. "Some I could help, others I tried to help and don't know what happened." She walked to the window where he stood. "Then there were those who didn't really want help. Those used to break my heart, but I learned to focus on the other two groups because at least there was a chance of saving them."

"I'd let you save me." Duncan wiggled his brows.

She rolled her eyes and pushed her glasses up once again. "You definitely don't need saving. You have your act together and then some." She turned and walked back to her chair, resting her hands on the back of it. "The problem was, when I was able to help, it was like an addiction. I must have produced endorphins that had me craving another success story until it was all I focused on. I guess you could say my job was my life."

"Did you no' have any fun?" The fake look of shock on his face almost had her laughing, but she kept her humor inside.

"Of course I did." She tried to bring up memories of good times and they all seemed to stem around her work. The Christmas parties for client children, the "retreat" to the beach for the staff, even the night she won twelve-hundred dollars playing bingo was at a fundraiser for those her agency helped.

"What did you do for yourself?"

She snapped her gaze to his. It was as if he'd read her mind. "Let's see." She dug deeper in her memory bank, back to before she was engaged when all they did was watch movies on television. "Oh, I dated some. I went bowling, to an amusement park…" She gave him a wink. "I even went to the highland games in New Hampshire."

He raised his brow at that. "Really?"

"Yes. I found the men at those more appealing than my date." She gave him a grin of her own. "Ended up going there every year with my friends before I moved out of state."

"Good. Then there may be hope for you after all." Duncan strode forward and grabbed her hands.

She frowned. "What do you mean?"

His chuckle had her insides melting all over again.

"I mean, lass, I'm pleased to learn you are open to a little fun now and again because I think you need a lot more than you had while alive. But right now we should continue Holly's journey. We dinna want to disappoint Cameron."

"Or Holly." She gave him a stern look. Once again he'd distracted her. He was dangerous to her profession and to her body. Luckily, she was smart enough to know him for what he was and the chances of her heart getting involved were nil. She couldn't wait to see what other happy moments were in store for their client. Being the Spirit of Christmas Past was far more fun than her old job. Hopefully, it would be just as rewarding. She certainly hoped so.

Duncan had phased and waited for her to as well. When she'd done so, he grasped her hand and returned them to Holly.

Chapter Four

Duncan liked the feel of Jessica's hand in his. He liked kissing her even more, but he didn't like how his heart tripped when he held her. That, and her penchant for unwittingly making him reevaluate his own life and afterlife didn't sit well. It made him… uncomfortable.

As the Christmas tree and older couple appeared, he pushed aside his thoughts and focused on Holly. That's what Jessica did. The woman seemed to have a one-track mind. Too bad he and she tended to be on different tracks.

Holly floated over the shoulder of Mrs. Tinder as she stuck new tags on presents and handed them to her husband, who sat on the floor arranging them beneath the tree.

Jessica placed her hand on Holly's shoulder. "I'm so glad everything worked out for you."

Holly turned to her and grasped her in another hug. "I don't know how to thank you. You changed our lives that night."

She chuckled uncomfortably. "I didn't know that, but I'm happy I could help." She released Holly, but held both her hands. "I guess sometimes one small action can make all the difference."

He'd swear Holly's smile couldn't get any wider. "I'll say. Who knew a catastrophe would end up being the best thing to ever happen to us? If that fire hadn't hit, you wouldn't have helped us and we wouldn't have met the Tinders. It's weird to think of life like that, like a chain of events that could have gone so differently."

Jessica nodded and let go of Holly's hands. "I'm also pleased I was assigned as your Spirit of Christmas Past so I could see how perfectly everything turned out for you."

Once again Duncan was surprised by the difference in height between the two women. It didn't occur to him until now exactly how tall Jessica was. The lasses in his past were much shorter and the difference was obvious. The feel of Jessica's curvy body lying atop his had his cock moving. He'd had to get her off him before she noticed his growing erection. She would be a joy to have in his bed.

"Duncan, Holly is ready for her next memory." Jessica looked at him quizzically.

Blast, wrong time for dreaming. "Good. Take my hand, lass, and we shall see what we can find."

Once he had both their hands securely in his own, he took them high and soared over the treetops a bit before bringing them down through the roof of an old, but well taken care of cottage on a pond. As they drifted into the living room, a teenager lay on the couch watching TV by the light of the Christmas tree. A fire across the room made the scene very homey. Then the teenager coughed and grabbed a tissue to blow her nose.

Jessica raised her brow at him, but didn't scowl this time.

"Oh, this was the Christmas I had the flu." Holly floated toward herself. "Ugh, I was so sick, I didn't even go to school the whole last week. I missed the Christmas dance and parties. That was my junior year."

Holly's mom came in dressed in jeans and a pretty red sweater. "Honey, you have a visitor."

Another woman with very short dark hair walked in bundled up in a blue parka and boots. "How are you feeling, Holly?"

Both young Holly and older Holly yelled at the same time. "Mrs. Connors!"

The woman laughed, showing pretty white teeth. "I don't think you'll be so happy to see me when I show you what I brought."

Holly turned to him and Jessica. "That's my teacher. She was the best teacher I ever had. She's why I decided to go into business."

After Holly turned back to relive her memory, Duncan looked over at Jessica. She wasn't smiling. In fact she looked as if she was about to cry.

He reached over and grasped her hand. She looked at him and shook her head, even as she released his hand to remove her glasses and wipe her eyes.

He turned back to the scene to find Mrs. Connors explaining the classwork to the teenage Holly so she could catch up over the break.

Holly turned around to them. "I'd never been so happy to receive homework. I was acing her class and by doing that big pile she gave me over the break, I was able to keep my A. She always went above and beyond for her students."

"Did she ever come in with any bruises or cuts?" Jessica's tone was serious.

"Yes, now that you mention it. She told us she was a klutz, but it was more, wasn't it?"

Jessica nodded. "I'm afraid so. She was a victim of domestic violence. I finally convinced her to leave her husband and I settled her in at Willow Wood. But when I visited two weeks later, she'd left. They thought she went back to her husband."

Holly frowned. "I don't think so. I took her the next school year for Advanced Marketing and she wasn't Mrs. Connors anymore. She told us she divorced and remarried and to call her Mrs. Brennen."

"Really?" Hope and relief battled for supremacy in Jessica's face.

Holly nodded. "Yes. Did you know her long?"

"Not long enough. It had taken me almost a year to get her to leave her husband. I didn't even question the staff at Willow Wood when they told me where she went. My supervisor at the time didn't want us wasting time on what she called 'beyond help' cases, so unless Mrs. Connors contacted me, I couldn't continue to work with her." Jessica paused and glanced at him. "She never called."

Holly smiled, a full smile that crinkled her eyes. "I loved her so much. In fact, I almost became a teacher because she was so influential, but my mom kindly suggested I might make a little more money in the corporate world." Holly squinched her nose. "I never did feel comfortable there. I ended up working for smaller businesses, which was my happy place."

When Holly turned back to watch the proceedings, Duncan grabbed Jessica's hand. She needed to "process" this and so did he. What was Cameron up to? Something else was at foot here and he didn't like it.

He floated her up through the ceiling and out into the dark night. He'd thought to bring her to her house, but in mid-transition, he headed for his castle, a need to have her in his domain, urged him home.

Jessica was too surprised by Holly's revelation to question Duncan whisking her away again. These two cases she'd considered failures were not failures after all. Was it her perspective? Was it her tunnel vision on the job? Was it because she felt like she was the only one who could help people?

At her last thought, her stomach tightened. She shied away from where her mind wanted to go and instead looked around. Solidifying, she craned her neck as her gaze followed a wall over a twelve-foot door all the way up to what looked like a three-story ceiling. "Where are we?"

Duncan turned her toward the rest of the room. "My home." He opened his arm as if he gave her a precious present.

A fire crackled in a large stone fireplace, which had a woven rug before it. Set back from this were two large wooden chairs with cushions that made her think of medieval thrones. To the right was what had to be a twenty-foot table pushed up against a wall and above it hung a beautiful, giant tapestry of a nine-point stag standing in a forest. To the left was an open double doorway that revealed an even bigger table with at least forty chairs set at it. There were three other smaller doorways, one of which she glimpsed a stone spiral staircase.

She stared at Duncan. His smile was hesitant, as if he wasn't sure what she would think of his home. To see his usual confidence missing tugged at her heart. "This is huge."

His smile lifted up on one side as if embarrassed. "My forefathers didn't update this section, but I like the medieval feel of it. If you would be more comfortable in the sixteenth or eighteenth century wings, we can go there." He lifted his hands, palms up. "I'm afraid the wealth of the Montgomeries in the fifteenth and seventeenth centuries wasn't enough to add on additional sections, but to be honest, this thing is a monstrosity as it is."

She walked to the chairs before the fireplace and ran her hand over the carving of a thistle on the back. "I love it. I always wanted to go to Scotland. I planned to stay in one of those castles they renovated into a hotel." She strolled around the giant chair and pushed on the cushion with her hand then sat. "Wow, I feel like a queen."

Duncan finally moved, striding over to take the other chair. "I'm glad you like it."

She ran her hand along the chair arm carved as a lion. "I do." Feeling his gaze on her, she looked at him to find him not smiling and his eyes intent. "Why did you bring me here?"

He shrugged, but it wasn't the effortless motion he usually portrayed. This one appeared forced. "I thought you may want to talk about what you learned about Mrs. Connors."

Actually, she didn't and she turned her head away. "Are the clients and the Spirit Guides always so entwined?"

"No."

At his short response, she glanced at him again and found him brooding. He looked like a different person, like a man of power and control and her stomach flipped over. "What are you thinking?"

He had his chin resting on his right fist, his elbow set on the arm of the chair, and for a moment, she didn't think he would answer.

"I think there is more to our assignment than what Cameron told us."

This was a different side of Duncan and she liked it as much, if not more, than his fun side. Did that make her a bore?

"I think," he turned his serious gaze on her, "he's testing you. And I dinna like it."

Why did her heart speed up at the protective sound in his voice? She needed to get a hold of herself. "You mean a test to see if I'm good enough to go it alone as a Spirit Guide?"

He shook his head. "No, I determine when you can go on your own."

"You do?" That thrilled her and bothered her at the same time. "So after I finish with Holly, you make a decision based on how well I helped her? Talk about pressure."

Duncan finally smiled. "Oh, I never let a Guide go by him or herself after just one trip."

She started to take offense before she recognized the gleam in his eye. He was teasing her. Finding a new camaraderie with him, she lifted one eyebrow. "There's a first time for everything."

Duncan's laughter filled the room and sent tingles skittering across her skin. Maybe she did like the fun side better.

He winked. "Then again, if you aren't ready, I get to accompany you on your next assignment."

She caught her breath. It was clear that was his preference. But was it because he enjoyed her company or that he still didn't have faith in her abilities? She pushed her glasses up to hide her confusion.

Duncan stood and held out his hand. "Would you like to see more of this wing?"

Something in his look reminded her of an old pick-up line, *I'm an artist. Really. Would you like to see my sketches?* There was far more on his mind than just a tour and her body sensed his intent. Not sure how she felt about that, she hesitated and his smile faltered.

Oh, that was too much. What harm was there in seeing the place? "I'd love to."

The smile he gave her this time was genuinely honest. He loved his home and for some reason, he wanted her to like it, too. Not hard to do, considering it was a *castle*. He walked her to the stairway and too soon released her hand.

"Up you go, lass. To truly appreciate this pile of stone, you need to start at the top."

She nodded and lifted her skirt with both hands so she wouldn't trip on the narrow stairs. After two stories of going around the tight spiral, she felt dizzy and placed her foot too close to the center where the step was no more than a couple inches wide.

As she lost her balance, she dropped her skirt and threw her arms out to catch herself.

Duncan's strong arm wrapped around her as she fell back. "I've got ye, lass."

The sound of his deeper accent, combined with the rapid beating of her heart, caused her to melt into him. "Thank you." She barely got the words out, no more than a whisper.

"My pleasure." Duncan's breath tickled her ear as he spoke, sending awareness through every nerve ending.

Her body lit up like a Christmas tree. His hard chest against her back kept her safe while the heavy arm that held her lay just beneath her breasts. Could he feel her heartbeat? "I'm okay now."

Instead of loosening his hold, Duncan held her tighter. "Aye, that ye be." No sooner had his words passed her ear than his lips found the side of her neck and he kissed her.

Her whole body shivered at his touch.

He smiled against her skin then nuzzled her nape before taking a deep breath. "Ach, lass you smell of Christmas and tartness and everything good. It makes me want to eat ye up."

"Oh." His words formed an image in her mind of his deep-blue eyes looking up at her from between her legs, a crooked grin on his lips. Probably not what he meant at all, or was it?

His other hand snaked around her and unbuttoned the top button of her blouse.

She should stop him because…because…there was a reason, but her mind refused to grasp it.

And then his hand was on her skin, moving toward her right breast, his fingers sliding beneath the white satin of her bra cup to find her nipple.

Her sheath reacted, tightening even as it swelled. His two fingers began to play with her hard nub, squeezing, rolling, flicking it until moisture gathered in her folds. She arched into his hand even as he nibbled her earlobe, making every part of her hot. Maybe all his experience did have some benefit.

She pressed her left hand against the stone wall as the ache inside her grew.

Duncan's arm around her waist moved lower, and his hand sneaked under the waistband of her skirt, burrowing its way beneath her panties.

Her body was primed, ready. Reaching her other hand out, she grasped the curve of the center column of the stairway and tilted her hips toward his traveling fingers.

Duncan didn't disappoint her. He moved his hand lower, pushing through the hair covering her mons, moving over her clit to explore the wetness of her folds. One finger slipped inside her ready sheath.

He cupped her, his finger still buried deep inside, and pulled her pelvis back against him, the hard ridge of his cock pressing against her ass. His other hand covered her whole breast and squeezed her to him. "Ach, lass, I could take ye right here."

Her pulse, already beating fast, skipped a beat. She let go of the walls and grabbed both his wrists, pressing his hands into her.

His body shuddered. "But it's no' safe." Slowly, despite her grip, he moved his hands away from her breast and opening, though his right arm remained around her.

A whimper escaped her lips and she flushed that she'd been so obvious. Still, she was thankful for his arm as her knees were weak.

Duncan didn't say anything as they stood on the stair, both breathing hard. After a minute, her balance returned and she leaned forward. "I'm good."

His chuckle behind her as he let her go had her turning to look at him. He raised his brow. "I dinna know that yet." His devilish grin told her he planned to find out and he wasn't talking about how good she was as a Spirit Guide.

She turned forward again and started climbing, going a little slower. She didn't want to get dizzy again and end up back in his arms. Or maybe she did. No. He was a lover and she kept forgetting how arrogant he could be.

On the other hand, he'd been concerned for their safety.

She stifled a laugh. How could they get hurt if they were already dead? She sobered almost immediately. Duncan had been a spirit for a couple centuries and even he still thought like the living on occasion. Would she ever get used to this? Would this be her eternity? Like him, would she have no sense of how much time passed?

A yearning for more than this started in her chest. She didn't like the feeling. The afterlife was supposed to be peaceful, not difficult.

After passing the third floor with only one door in the side wall, she continued upward. How big was this place anyway? He said this was the medieval section but there were two other wings with the latest being the eighteenth century. Was that when he was from? What was happening in Scotland then?

The stairs opened to a small hallway with a wooden door at the end. She walked to it then turned back to look at Duncan.

He nodded. "Go ahead, open it." The anticipation in his face piqued her curiosity.

She lifted the latch, pushed the wooden door open and stepped out. "Oh wow." She stopped where she was and looked over the crenellated stone along the edge of the roof. Before her lay green rolling hills, some dotted with light purple, leading down to an ocean. "This is beautiful."

She looked at Duncan, who was also staring at the vista, and she could easily see him in a kilt and loose white shirt. His chin was up as the light breeze ruffled his hair. He looked like a lord or laird or whatever they were called when he was alive, as if he owned everything before him.

He turned toward her and grinned. "Welcome to Rossan."

"Where in Scotland is this?"

He cocked his head as he thought. "South of the River Clyde." He pointed. "That's the Atlantic ocean."

It looked like there was a village on the coast, but the cottages inland seemed scattered far apart from each other, not that she could see every hill and valley. "What time period is this? I'm guessing it's in the eighteenth century some time."

He shrugged and returned his gaze to the scenery.

He really couldn't remember. She wanted him to. For some reason that was important. "Did you wear kilts?"

He turned to face her and leaned back against the stone edge, crossing his legs. "Aye, I did and I do." His smile faltered before it grew wider. "My father wasn't allowed to, some idiot law, but I remember wearing the Montgomerie plaid from as far back as when I was a wee boy."

She tried to envision what the six foot six Mr. Distraction looked like as a child. Surprisingly, it wasn't that hard. He would have been precocious, always laughing and probably getting into all kinds trouble. She smiled at the image.

"Ah, you have figured it out then?" He winked, but his smile didn't reach his eyes.

Her instincts were finally helping her see the slight nuances in his face. She'd been distracted by the smiles and laughter, but now, she could see that sometimes those were used to hide doubts and dare she think it, insecurities.

She sauntered over to him. "As a matter of fact, I have."

"Then please enlighten this old soul." He bowed his head slightly in respect, not in fun.

She squelched a flirtatious reply. "I believe you were born around 1780."

"Why is that?"

"I'm no expert, but I was supposed to take a trip to Scotland and did a little research. The Scots always wanted to be separate from the English crown and in the 1700s there was an attempt to put a Bonnie Stuart on the throne."

"Aye." His face lit with excitement. "Bonnie Prince Charlie."

She frowned. "But that failed and the English king outlawed the wearing of the kilt, playing the bagpipes and basically anything truly Scottish."

Duncan stood straight, now clearly remembering. "That's why my father couldn't wear a kilt, but then they repealed the law. That's why I could. You're brilliant."

With no warning, he scooped her into his arms and kissed her. This wasn't the sensual kiss on her couch. This was a full on, overpowering assault on her senses as his tongue entwined with her own and his body pressed her against the pitched roof.

His hand cupped her head as he slanted his lips across hers like a man starved. Her soul took notice and she wrapped her arms around his neck, burying her hands in his thick hair.

Just when she thought her knees would give way, he retreated, but not far. He leaned his forehead against hers and with his finger traced her swollen lips.

"I'm sorry, lass. I canna control myself around ye."

Every feminine part of her cheered at his statement even as she noticed his Scottish accent had become heavier. "Hmm, I'm thinking that happens with every girl you kiss."

He lifted his head and stared into her eyes, all traces of amusement gone. "Nay, it does no'. Ye are the first."

Oh, sheesh. This wasn't what she'd expected. How did he completely flip the tables on her? She moved her hand to his cheek. "You're pretty awesome, too."

Instead of laughing, or at least a smile, he frowned. He didn't say a word, turned his head and kissed her palm.

What was he thinking?

Duncan didn't want to let Jessica go, even for a moment, and panic crowded upon him. He didn't understand why he, the man who had lain with women in more than a hundred beds, though to be truthful they weren't all in beds, but still, why couldn't he stop thinking of her. It bothered him enough to walk away, but his body refused to budge.

"Duncan? Are you all right?"

Ignoring her question, he listened to his body and lowered his lips to hers again. As soon as they touched, lightning crashed inside him, making his balls tighten and his cock hard. Her breasts, pressing against his chest, burned him and he couldn't keep his hands from moving over her.

He wanted to kiss every part of this woman. Every stubborn, sassy, smart inch of her. He forced his lips to move away from her sweet mouth to her neck, which he'd tasted on the stairs.

She leaned her head away, giving full access to that smooth white column where her pulse beat so diligently. He licked at it before kissing his way to her collarbone, his fingers deftly popping another button open on her blouse.

The soft fabric moved away as his mouth descended on the crest of a breast and he tongued the skin above the bra. Following the lace edging downward with his lips to the space between her breasts, he licked between them all the way up to the hollow at her throat.

Her scent wafted around him as her pulse beat rapidly beneath his tongue. He craved her.

Taking a deep breath, he inhaled her cranberry aroma, the fresh air of the day, and the tiniest whiff of salt air from the sea. He moved his lips to her ear. "I want ye, Jess."

Lifting his head to see her response, he found her staring at him through half-closed eyes that had turned darker than the evergreens in the distance. As carefully as he could, he lifted the glasses from her face, fascinated by the lighter green flecks visible in her eyes. "Ye are so bonny, lass. I canna help myself."

Need as well as hesitancy was clear in her gaze. He didn't want her to think. He wanted her to feel. With his elbows anchored against the slope of the roof, he lowered his head and gently kissed her, holding back his raging need to woo her body into submission.

Lazily, he explored her sweet taste, his cock hardening as her tongue finally tangled with his own. His hips pressed against her of their own accord and she moaned into his mouth at his movement. He burrowed his knee between her legs, nudging them apart.

Without leaving her delicious mouth, he balanced on one elbow and released his hard cock from the stifling denim. His hope was that with it open to the fresh air instead of confined in the pants they called jeans, he would have more control, but he was mistaken.

He had to have her. From her reaction on the stairs and her moans now, she must be ready for him. Leaving her lips, he nuzzled between her breasts before forcing his tongue beneath her bra and tugging on her nipple. Bracing his legs, he used one hand to pull down the material and grasp her breast in his hand, kneading it, loving the soft firmness of it.

Over the thudding of his own heart, he focused on the small gasps of air she took. She wanted him. He wanted her. There was no reason to wait. Removing his hand from her breast, he hiked up her skirt to her waist until he could press his cock against her.

Blast, there was still yet another barrier before him. It was too much clothing. With his hand, he pulled the underthing to the side and thrust inside her silky sheath.

"Duncan. Duncan!" He'd just registered her voice when a sting from a slap spread across his face.

"What?"

"Where did you go? One minute we're having a conversation and the next minute you're in Never Never Land."

Huh? He stared at Jessica. Her blouse only had the one button undone, she still wore her glasses and she was standing in front of him as he leaned against the stone crenellation. What happened?

"Duncan, are you okay?"

A pressure in the back of his head built. He looked into her worried eyes, knowing his own must reveal the same. "Aye, lass, I'm fine." But he wasn't fine and she probably knew it. "Would you like to see more of this wing?" He turned away from her and rubbed at the pressure at the base of his skull, the pain increasing. Confused by what happened and by her caring, he pointed below instead. "Or I can show you one of the other ones."

She walked around him and placed her hands on her hips. "No, I don't want to see the other wings. I want to know what happened just now. I was talking to you for at least ten minutes and you didn't respond. It was like you were a zombie or something."

A shiver raced through his body at her words. Whispers of spirits who disappeared, vanishing into nothingness from being around too long sliced through his brain as the pressure in his skull blew apart and he grasped his head in his hands.

Chapter Five

"Duncan!" Jessica grabbed his arms, easing the sharpness a bit, but he barely kept himself upright.

He opened his eyes to the loveliness of her face, and the pain dulled a bit more. "Sorry, lass. Just got a wee bit of a headache."

"Then we should go downstairs. Can you phase?"

He grasped her hand, no' sure if he could. "I'm the expert at phasing. They really should have let me do that training for new Spirit Guides."

She rolled her eyes, but her concern didn't leave her face. "Then let's go, Mr. Expert."

As his body obeyed his command to phase, he breathed easier, the pain easing and pooling into a puddle at the base of his skull. They floated down the outside of the building and through the front door. By time they re-solidified and he sat at the huge banquet table while Jessica searched the kitchen for the ale he requested, he was feeling more like himself, the ache in his head all in one spot but manageable.

"Here you go." She set a ceramic mug before him and took the seat next to him.

He wasn't oblivious to the fact her hand rested on his arm. He picked up the mug with his other hand and took a swallow then grimaced. "That's no' ale."

She grinned. "Nope. It's orange juice. I requested it. If you had a drop in blood sugar or lightheadedness then that will cure you in no time."

He doubted that. "And how do you know this?"

"My grandmother swore by the miracles worked through OJ. Now drink some more."

He made a face at her for the fun of it and took another swallow. It was good.

Her brows drew together. "Haven't you had orange juice before?"

"No. I've had oranges." He smiled as a childhood memory struck him. "When I was a boy, my parents used to hide oranges at Christmas time. My little brother and I loved looking for them. My parents would give us clues that would take us hours to figure out and when we did, it would still take hours to find the blasted things." He winked at her. "I think it was just their way of keeping us occupied while the servants decorated the house."

Jessica smiled in return. "That sounds like a wonderful memory." She could see him sitting in that chair he was in, but less than half the size. Probably feeding anything he didn't want to eat to the family dog, swinging his bare feet as he pretended to listen. Except maybe not bare feet. She looked at his tartan-colored socks. "Why don't you wear shoes?"

He wiggled his brow. "Because I misbehaved."

"You, really?" She chuckled. "What a surprise. So how did misbehaving stop you from wearing shoes?"

He grimaced. "It was my fault, of course. I was sliding down the banister in the eighteenth century portion of the house when I fell."

"Oh no." Her breath caught.

"Obviously, I lived that day." He winked. "Luckily, I fell on the stair side and no' on the two-story-drop side."

She started breathing again. "You must have been scared."

"I was at first. I was just a wee boy, maybe five. But when I landed on the stairs I thought all was well. All I needed to do was get my feet out from between the spindles. What I didn't know is I had broken my ankle and when I tried to move to untie my shoes so I could get my feet loose, it hurt. So I just hung there, head first off one stair hoping one of the servants or my older brother would find me."

"Didn't they hear you crying?" Her heart went out to the naughty boy, Duncan had been.

He shook his head proudly. "I was a boy. I couldn't cry. And I wouldn't yell for help because I really didn't want my parents to find out I was sliding down the banister again."

"Wait, so you thought if someone else found you, they wouldn't tell your parents about your ankle."

He chuckled. "I didn't know about my ankle, and yes, in my mind, I could convince whoever found me to keep my secret."

Jessica leaned forward. "Who found you?"

He grimaced again. "Me mum."

She laughed at that. "But what does that have to do with not wearing shoes?"

Duncan took another swallow of juice before he answered, the gleam in his eye telling her she would adore his response. "At first my foot swelled so badly I couldn't wear shoes, and my father delayed my punishment since I couldn't walk. Then as my foot got better, I had become so comfortable no' wearing shoes that I kicked them off the first chance I got. My nanny thought it was because my 'wee poor foot' bothered me. I never disabused her of that idea. Before I knew it, my shoeless life was looked upon as normal, even by me. Besides," he wiggled his toes in his socks, "socks keep your feet warm and are much more comfortable than shoes."

Jessica shook her head. "I had a feeling you were a little scamp as a boy."

"Me?" He tried to look affronted. "What makes you think that?"

She raised an eyebrow and cocked her head. "Are you sure you want me to answer that?"

Oh, he liked the deviltry in her gaze. She had spirit, more than he'd guessed. "Aye. What makes you think I was a troublemaker?"

"Oh, let me count the ways." She bowed, one arm straight out, then she rose. "Hmm, well first you smile all the time."

"That's my good humor. Certainly a plus. I make people happy with this smile." He smiled widely to prove his point.

Her lips quirked up a bit at the sides as she tried not to reciprocate. "Second," she paced to the left, "you like to tease."

He folded his arms across his chest. "Again, a good quality. I make people laugh, which makes them feel good."

She shook her head, refusing his logic. She paced to the right. "Third, you are an outrageous flirt."

"All the better for enjoying a tryst or two." He winked at her before letting his gaze roam over her body.

"Two? I'm thinking there's been more than two." She smirked at him, finally relaxing and having fun.

He grinned, filled with male satisfaction. "Aye, it's probably closer to two hundred."

Jessica's face froze. "Really?"

He shrugged. "I dinna know. I never counted. But that too brings pleasure to others."

Jessica stared at the smiling man in front of her, forcing herself to keep her mouth shut as numerous names for Duncan Montgomerie raced through her head. *Lady-killer. Casanova. User. Player. Heartbreaker.* Her mind stopped on the last one. She'd almost forgotten that about him. How many women back in his time had loved him, only to be tossed aside for the next willing wench?

He still grinned. "So again, I ask you, why would you think I was a troublemaker when I was younger?" He smiled in triumph as if he'd argued away all her points when in fact he brought up a much worse one.

Did he seriously not see the issue with two hundred sex partners? Far be it for her to explain it. "I stand corrected." She pivoted on her heel and walked toward the door.

"Where are you going?" His voice made it sound as if he cared.

She didn't turn around. "I need to go back to my house. I'll come get you when I'm ready to continue Holly's night.

"Jessica."

She phased, ignoring the entreaty in his voice and floated to her home on the Maine inlet. When she entered, she immediately solidified and went straight to the freezer. She pulled out the ice cream and a spoon and went outside, hoping Duncan wouldn't follow her. She just needed some time to think.

Scooping out a heaping spoonful, she stuffed it in her mouth. At the sweet taste of cherries, she glanced at the carton. It wasn't pistachio. Sheesh, she couldn't even grab the right ice cream. Not about to get out of the comfortable rocking chair, she shrugged and took another bite. Cherry vanilla was pretty good too. It was no replacement for Duncan Montgomerie's kiss, but it would have to do.

She stabbed the spoon in again. What had she been thinking in the stairway? The man was focused on only one thing when it came to women. Sure, she'd seen other sides to him, but what kind of man boasted of sleeping with two hundred women?

She stilled. Had those all been when he was alive? If that were the case, he had to have slept with…if he was thirty-six and didn't start having sex until he was sixteen, that would be ten a year!

She spooned out another heaping teaspoon of ice cream and stuffed it in her mouth. But what if those women included ones he'd had sex with in the afterlife? On one hand, that would be better as that would bring the count down to less than one a year. But on the other hand, if he was as promiscuous in the afterlife, that meant she could run into one of his former sex partners. She didn't like that scenario at all.

Why not? Why should she care if he slept around? It wasn't like she wanted to have sex with him. *Liar.* Okay, she was attracted to him and from the episode on the stairs, he could turn her on in a heartbeat. Shit, she'd known he would be a distraction. She should be focusing on Holly, not herself.

Even at that thought, the memory of Duncan's concern over her and Holly's entwined lives had her heart softening. She wanted to believe he cared about her enough to protect her, but she didn't even know from what. What threat could there be in the afterlife?

It was so complicated, which made sense as she was new to it all. Then again, how new was she? It sounded like she'd been here for at least five years or more. So why didn't she know more? The fact that Duncan, who'd been in the afterlife over two hundred years, was not only baffled by her and Holly's entwined lives, but concerned, made her nervous. Did that mean there were worse things than death? A shiver ran through her body that had nothing to do with the ice cream in her hands.

She took another bite, crunching down on a whole maraschino cherry. Its sweetness was heavenly, but she could only taste it when solid. Why was there this dual existence? She wasn't a ghost, unwilling to leave the living, yet she wasn't all spirit, at least she didn't feel like it. Was there another realm or was the list of jobs she'd seen all there was to eternity?

No matter how the afterlife was configured, she still needed Duncan to get through this assignment. He knew more than she did, even if he didn't know why Cameron was testing her. Then again, he didn't appear to know what had happened to him on the roof.

The image of Duncan's faraway stare floated across her mind. Her stomach knotted. That wasn't right either. It was as if he'd left his body. She hadn't seen anyone else like that and he'd definitely been surprised, maybe even a little fearful. And since when did spirits get headaches?

She scraped the bottom of the ice cream container. Good thing she only kept the two pint containers. If left to her own devices, she'd probably finish a whole gallon and wonder if there was more.

Feeling a little better now that she'd had her favorite food and time to mull over her current existence, she should return to Duncan and continue Holly's journey. At least he might be able to answer some of her questions. He was her mentor after all. She just needed to remember that was all he was and not get sidetracked by Mr. Distraction.

She finally rose and walked into her kitchen to throw out the container and leave the spoon in the sink. When she turned around, she jumped.

Duncan stood in her kitchen. "I apologize. I dinna mean to startle you."

Jessica put her hand to her heart. He'd scared the life out of her. Uh, except she didn't have any in her. "You really need to learn to knock."

She tried to go around him, but he grabbed her arm. "Jessica. I'm sorry."

"It's okay. I imagine I need to get used to it."

He looked away for a moment before meeting her gaze. "No, I mean about what I said. I doubt I have been with that many women. I did no' actually count. I promise you I did no' play with their affections if that concerns you. I was always very forthright that I could no' love them. It's just no' in me. They understood it was just for enjoyment."

She pulled away, her chest tightening to hear him say he could not love. It was too sad to contemplate. She didn't want to think about him anymore. She'd never expected him to be Mr. Distraction in an emotional way as well.

Determined to keep their relationship as professional as possible, she shrugged. "It doesn't matter. It's none of my business." She walked into the living room. "Besides, we've had a long break and probably should get back to Holly."

"No' yet." He came in and motioned for her to take a seat.

Maybe this would be another lesson in what not to do. This time she'd listen. It bothered her she'd missed so much of what he said in training because she was too busy daydreaming about getting him into bed. What a waste of time that had been. It was the last place she wanted him now.

He strode to her couch and sat. Though he smiled, it was one of those he used for just for show. "Tell me about Mrs. Connors."

She stiffened. "I don't want to talk about her."

"Why?"

She pushed her glasses up her nose as she gathered her thoughts. Mrs. Connors had been one of her failures, firmly categorized in that column. She spent her entire career trying to make the successes double that of her failures. But what if some of her failures had been successes? Had she wasted her own life to help others who didn't need help?

Or worse yet, what if her successes ended up failures and she never knew. Her whole reason for living was in doubt. Not an easy thing to explain to a man who skated along the top of life, enjoying what it offered and not worrying about others' lives. She didn't blame him necessarily. After all, he was helping people now. She'd seen his compassion toward Holly. Was that why he was a mentor, to make up for what he didn't do in life? If so, then why was she accepted as a Spirit Guide? Was it a reward or something else?

"Lass, what is it?"

She refocused on him and found his brow lowered in worry. His obvious concern loosened her throat. "It's everything. It's this place, your castle, the phasing abilities, the helping Holly. I'm just confused. And uncertain, which I'm not used to being. I always knew what to do, or I thought I did. Now I'm discovering I didn't know the half of it."

He didn't smile or tease her, which made it clear he was seriously listening, but it also added to her worries.

"My gut says there is something more to this than simply helping Holly." He paused, but then clearly had made a decision. "If there is one more incident with a connection between you two, I'm going to Cameron to demand some answers."

Usually she was happy to fight her own battles, after all, she always had. Whether it was getting her boss to let her go one step further with a case, needling someone into helping a client, or persisting to a judge that a child would be better off back with its parent, she'd always fought for what was right. But the afterlife was different, and she didn't know her way around it yet. Having Duncan promising to look out for her did make her feel better. He may be a happy guy, but he had a lot more experience than she did.

"Thank you. I would appreciate that. I know we're supposed to be helping Holly dispel some of her sorrow, but these connections are really messing with my head."

"Messing with your head?"

She grinned. "Sorry, it's a silly expression. It means it's driving me crazy. No, I mean—"

Duncan raised his hand and his smile was back. "I understand. I've had students who explained what driving one crazy means."

"Is it hard keeping up with the phrases and technology and clothing and just everything?"

"Aye, it would give me a headache if I could get them."

"But you said you just had one." Had he lied to her?

He grimaced. "I am no' sure what that was." He winked. "Guess I'll just have to ask Cameron about that as well next time I see him."

He pretended to shrug off what happened to him, but she recognized his almost-smiles now. He was concerned. Good, she'd seen the glaze in his eyes and he did need to take his "headache" seriously. If they were alive, she'd tell him to see a doctor. Who did you see about anomalies in the afterlife?

Duncan stood, phasing even before he'd risen to his full height. "Ready?"

She couldn't do that yet, two things at once, so she phased then stood. "Yes. Let's go make Holly happy."

He grinned and took her hand.

As they flew through time and space together, her need to be perfect at her new job on the first try lessened. If she was, then she'd be doing this by herself and she wouldn't see Duncan much, or could she? Why would she? If being a Spirit Guide was anything like being a social worker, she wouldn't have time.

But there was no time in the afterlife. Did that mean she could do everything? That excited and frightened her at the same time. She'd better stick to focusing on her client and grapple with the other possibilities later. She'd already spent far too much of her energy on Duncan and herself. Her job was to help Holly.

"…for smaller businesses which was my happy place." Holly pointed to a jar of jellybeans on the coffee table. "Even then I worked part time for a Jelly Bean Gift Shop. I think my mom was more excited about me working there than I was. She loved jelly beans, especially tart ones. I was more into the tropical flavors. I always wanted to go to a Caribbean island, but the year I went with friends to the Bahamas for spring break during college cured me of that fantasy."

Duncan let go of Jessica's hand when she released his, but he didn't want to. He liked having her with him and no' just because she was beautiful. He liked her company.

Jessica, smart woman that she was, jumped into the conversation as if they'd never left. "Why did that cure you of wanting to go to an island?"

Holly shook her head. "Ugh, it was nothing but a drink fest. Everyone was drinking, 'hooking up,' and getting sick. I still can't think of a beach without getting queasy."

"You drank that much?"

"No." Holly's eyes widened. "Not me. But you can only see so much vomit before you start feeling sick yourself. I actually took a taxi to the airport eight hours before our flight was to leave just to get away from the scene."

Jessica stared at Holly. "That makes sense. I wouldn't have pegged you for a party girl. Guess us boring types need to stick together." She winked.

"Do you think we would have been friends if we met again later after I was an adult?" Holly looked at Jessica with curiosity.

"Definitely. I would have liked you right away, just like I did when I met you tonight."

"That's right." Holly looked at him. "It's still Christmas Eve, right?"

"Yes it is, and we have more to show you. Would you like to go to the next stop?"

Holly looked back at her younger self conversing with her favorite teacher. She sighed. "Yes, I'm ready."

Duncan held out his hand and she grasped it, then he took Jessica's in his other, no' questioning why he didn't put Holly between them. He floated them out of the cottage and to the next Christmas Eve in Holly's life.

He hoped she was ready for it. They hadn't given her a lot of time to ponder some of the happy points in her life, something he usually did. His interest in Jessica had thrown off his usual routine. Maybe that's why Cameron didn't assign him women very often. Smart man.

After the next stop, he'd bring Holly outside and have a conversation about her experience so far. Or better yet, he'd let Jessica have that conversation. It was obvious the two women had bonded. As long as their connection wasn't too strong, there was no need to worry about it and every reason it could help.

He floated them over snow-covered mountains and into a small village sandwiched between them.

As they drew closer, Holly pointed with her free hand. "Who are they?"

He looked to where she pointed and glanced at Jessica, who shrugged. Didn't the woman remember anything from his training? He shook his head before addressing Holly. "Those are ghosts. You can tell by how faded they are and the way they never stop moving."

Both women grasped his hands tighter as he brought them to hover over what appeared to be an old woman in a short cape and scarf floating down the road. She turned into a small house and at the same time, from within that house, a young female ghost slipped out the back and headed for the wooded property surrounding it.

"Can they see us?" Holly looked at him, her gaze nervous.

"No' usually. They are on a different plane. Once in a while a recent ghost will still be able to see us, but since they are tied to the living, after years go by, they can't anymore."

Jessica watched the young woman ghost, her eyes concerned. "Their clothing must be centuries old."

He shrugged. "I think that is late 1800s dress, but I am no' sure. I am no expert on women's clothes." Though he was very good at getting women out of them.

Jessica frowned at him as if she'd read his thoughts and he winked.

When she snapped her head back toward the forest, he chuckled and squeezed Holly's hand. "I dinna think Jessica believes me."

Holly grinned. "I wonder why?"

He laughed as he directed them back above the rooftops.

Holly tugged on his hand. "Wait a minute. How come I could see you in my house, but the Tinders and Mrs. Connors couldn't see us?"

"Very perceptive. Jessica, did you wish to answer this?"

Jessica shook her head. "You're the expert."

Doubt about how much Jessica had actually learned in his training grew and it concerned him, but he pasted on a smile for Holly. "The reason is because when Cameron came to you, he enabled you to see spirits. But dinna worry, after midnight tonight, you won't be able to see them anymore.

"Even Cameron?" Holly's sudden tension tugged at his heart.

"That's up to Cameron. He can let you see spirits whenever he chooses, but just remember, if you can see spirits, you can see ghosts and no' all of them are as mundane as the two we just came across."

"As long as I can see Cam, I don't care."

He swore she would have crossed her arms if he wasn't holding her hand. The lass didn't know what she truly wished for. The living never did.

A distant memory knocked at the back of his head. A wish. While he lived. He had wished for something. But as he tried to focus on it, it skittered away like a frightened wee mousie. No' that it mattered. He was no' living anymore. He looked over Holly's head at Jessica. No he wasn't and he was perfectly happy where he was.

Floating over the town, he finally brought them down into the second floor of an old Victorian house that had been converted into four small apartments. He stopped in the living room, fully decorated for Christmas. The lass had obviously always loved Christmas.

Holly gasped. "Oh, this was my place in Littleton." She floated around the empty room and hovered next to the tree. "I still have this ornament. My mother bought it for me for my eighteenth birthday. And this one I got from Grandma Tinder. Now it has a crack in it. When we got Mac, or rather when he adopted us, he batted it off the tree and broke it. I glued it together."

Duncan glanced at Jessica. She had a warm smile on her face. At least the apartment wasn't familiar.

The sound of footsteps coming toward the living room had them all holding their breath.

"We have plenty of nuts, Holly. I'll just grab them from the hor d'oeuvres tray in the living room." Cameron Douglas entered the room, heading for a round plastic tray set out on a coffee table.

Holly gasped, her gaze glued to the young Cameron.

"Don't you dare." The younger Holly strode into the room and swatted Cameron's hand. "Those are for the guests."

"Ow." He grabbed his hand and held it to his chest. "But the cookies are for the guests too and you said you needed more peanuts."

Young Holly crossed her arms, oblivious to the food stains on her full-length apron. "I would have had enough nuts if someone hadn't been eating them behind my back all week."

Cameron grinned and scooped her into his embrace. "Holly love, I needed the protein. You've been wearing me out. I didn't think a little midnight snack would upset your holiday plans."

She smiled. "That is so not fair, Cam."

"I know." He winked before he lowered his head and gave her a sweet kiss.

Duncan looked over at Holly. She had tears in her eyes. He certainly hoped Cameron knew what he was doing here.

When the kiss ended, young Holly batted at Cameron's shoulder. "As much as I'd like to spend the evening kissing you, we have company coming. So why don't you bring that tray into the kitchen and find something to replace the peanuts with."

"Aye, hen, if you insist." Cameron let her go, but as she turned, he swatted her ass and she spun back on him and frowned.

"Watch your hands, young man."

He just grinned at her until her lips twitched and she shook her head. Without another word, she sashayed out of the room.

Cameron's gaze was wolfish until she was out of sight, then it changed. His hand found his chest and the love in his eyes was so strong Duncan looked away.

Holly started to cry in earnest and Jessica flew to her side, wrapping her in her arms.

He tried to keep his optimism. "Why are you crying?"

Jessica scowled at him. "Because she misses him, why else?"

"No, that's not why." Holly's head came up. "I'm crying because I just remembered what happens to my Christmas Eve dinner. It was a total disaster and we had company. I was so embarrassed."

Jessica let go. "You were crying over your failed dinner?"

Holly wiped her eyes with her sleeve. "Yeah, I was trying so hard to impress Cameron and his friends and I totally blew it."

Jessica looked at him in confusion.

He floated across the room. "Cameron specifically wanted you to see this night, Holly. Why do you think that is?" He smiled encouragingly.

She sniffed. "I don't know."

"Come, lass. Think about it."

She looked around the room then shrugged. "Maybe because in the end it really didn't mean much."

Duncan nodded. "Aye. Cameron loved you for you, no' for your skills or ability to impress his friends."

Holly's lips twitched up. "We did laugh about this night every year. He said I improved with age."

Jessica grinned. "What a sweetheart."

Holly nodded, pride in her face. "He was and he was mine."

"He still is." Jessica squeezed Holly's shoulders.

There was a knock on the door and Cameron left the room, the tray in his hand. When he returned, two couples joined him.

Jessica's smile disappeared and Duncan stared at the newcomers. What the blazes was going on now?

Chapter Six

Holly had turned at the new arrivals, oblivious to Jessica's shock. "Oh wow, there's Tommy and Hannah and that's Jacob and his girlfriend of the hour. I don't remember her name. We never knew who he would bring."

Duncan watched as Jessica's fists clenched before she spoke, her voice rough. "When was this?"

Holly didn't turn. "It was five years ago. It was Cameron's and my first Christmas together. He took two weeks holiday, as he called it, to spend Christmas and New Year's with me." She pointed to one of the men. "We always invited Tommy to Christmas Eve dinner because if he hadn't brought Cameron to the Highland games earlier that year, we would never have met."

Holly glanced at Duncan. "The other guy was a friend of Tommy's. We saw him a few times after that, always with a different woman, but even Tommy got tired of him."

The look on Jessica's face proved she barely kept herself from solidifying and telling Jacob what she thought. That sent a slice of fear straight up Duncan's spine. He leaned toward Holly. "I need to talk to Jessica outside. Do you mind waiting here?"

Holly shook her head before glancing back at Jessica. "Oh, of course. I'll wait right here."

"Good lass." He floated to Jessica and grabbed her arm.

She looked about to argue but he shook his head and pulled her outside.

A light snow was falling and the moon reflected off the white blanket covering the rooftops and trees. It gave Jessica the appearance of a silver angel and something in Duncan's heart shifted.

She apparently didn't feel like an angel as she floated back and forth across the roof. "That son of a bitch. And here I felt guilty for putting off the wedding."

He didn't say anything. The second Holly had mentioned the name Jacob, he knew in his gut it was Jessica's fiancé. Too many emotions had roiled through him—jealousy, anger and protectiveness. But he'd had little chance to examine the man because fear had overtaken everything. Fear she'd solidify. What in the blazes was Cameron doing?

"And Tommy." Jessica threw up her hands as she floated. "How could he? He introduced me to that bastard."

Duncan's concern grew. "You know Tommy too?"

"Of course I knew Tommy. We worked together in Maine. Oh…" She slowed to face him. "I'm the one who told Tommy about the New Hampshire Highland Games when he said he had a friend visiting from Scotland. That friend must have been Cameron."

Duncan's fear for her was turning to anger at Cameron now. It was time the man answered some questions.

Jessica's hand on his arm had him swallowing his curse.

"I always wondered if I'd made the right decision. I accepted a job in Maine that paid me more money and a promotion, but I always felt like maybe I'd abandoned the people back in New Hampshire. But I would never have met Tommy if I didn't and if I hadn't told Tommy about the games, Holly would have never met Cameron."

She stared at him, her eyes wide. "I never realized how connected we all are." She attempted to smile. "Maybe if we try hard enough, we can find a connection between us."

Duncan couldn't keep from touching her a moment longer. He pulled her into his embrace. His heart raced with fear and he wanted to confront it, but he had no idea what the threat was. "This is no coincidence. Cameron knew you were key to him meeting Holly. What I want to know is why he's revealing this to you. He should be focused on making Holly happy. I dinna like it."

Jessica rested her head against his shoulder. "I'm so glad this isn't the normal way these assignments go. I don't think I could handle a hundred different cases that revealed so many of my past assumptions were wrong."

He held her tight, liking the feel of her against him, but for once no' in a sexual capacity. She was being put through an emotional cider press as if she were a living person in need of redemption, but he'd never met a more caring soul in his entire afterlife. She didn't need redemption.

Something inside him told him to stay with her if he wanted to keep her safe, but he had to speak to Cameron if he wanted to discover what was in store for them in order to protect her. That Cameron hadn't told Duncan the full plan had him skunnered.

He leaned his head back and lifted her chin. "Jess, I need to find out what Cameron is planning. I dinna want you taken by surprise again. If you had solidified…" He swallowed the lump in his throat. "It's time Cameron told us what his real goal is with this assignment."

"Good idea. Let's go."

"No, I dinna think he'll tell me if you are with me."

Jessica nodded and pulled out of his arms. He forced himself to let her go, his gut tight over what was the right course of action. "Do you want to wait in your house, maybe have more ice cream?"

She gave him a scowl. "Are you saying I'm fat?"

"No. You're perfect."

"Duncan, I was kidding. No, I'll stay here with Holly."

There was no way he'd allow that with her former fiancé present. If she stayed with Holly it would be *after* Jacob was long gone. He doubted her ability to keep from solidifying. She was far too angry at the man, which he didn't mind in the least. "Very well, but whatever happens, dinna solidify. Promise?"

She nodded.

He took her hand, moving them through time a few hours and into the apartment where Holly stood watching her former self cuddle with Cameron on the couch, all the company long gone.

"I'll be right back, lassies." With a last look at Jessica, he floated aloft as fast as he could, already anxious to return.

Jessica put her arm around Holly's shoulders. She needed to focus on making Holly happy, not on her own revelations. "How are you doing?"

Holly turned to her. "I'm good. It was so great to see us together like this. Everything was so simple. It only became complicated when we decided to get married. The whole quandary of which country to hold the wedding in, or to have two weddings or one in one country and again in another country. It got so crazy, we finally went to Vegas and eloped."

Jessica smiled, happy to focus on Holly's marriage instead of her own close call in marrying a jerk. "How did your families take the news?"

"Remarkably well. We did end up having receptions on both continents. Oh, you should have seen the party Grandma and Grandpa Tinder threw for us. It was a celebration of our marriage, but also a going away party because I was moving to Scotland permanently."

"Was that difficult?"

"Yes and no. It was hard leaving my friends and family, but I had Cam." Holly sighed as she looked back at him. "I would have gone anywhere with him."

Jessica laid her hand on Holly's shoulder. "You were very lucky to have found each other. Many people live very long lives having never known the kind of love you two shared."

The other woman snapped her head around. "You're right. I never thought of it that way."

Jessica nodded, barely keeping her own tears at bay. Even her own illusion that she had found love had been stripped away.

"Oh, Jessica. I'm being so selfish. I didn't realize Jacob was your fiancé. I just heard him telling Cam about you. Once Cam heard that, we stopped inviting him. We were disgusted."

She shook her head, refusing to shed any more tears over her life. If she'd learned anything so far, it was that most of what she'd believed was wrong. "It's okay. This is not about me, but about you."

"Still, I'm glad you never married the asshole."

Jessica grinned. She'd forgotten how nice it was to have a girlfriend to commiserate with. She'd had one while she lived in New Hampshire, but once she moved out of state, she hadn't been able to keep in touch and never found time to form a new friendship. With Holly, she clicked right away, but that may have been because she thought of her as a client first. "I guess delaying the wedding had been the smartest thing I did. Maybe in my subconscious I knew he wasn't the right one for me."

"So is Duncan the right one?"

She stared at Holly as if she'd just sprouted antlers and turned into a reindeer. "Why in the world would you say that?" She put as much shock into her voice as she could, though something too close to her heart waited anxiously for the answer.

Holly crossed her arms. "I don't know, it's just something about the way you two react to each other. It reminds me of the Tinders, only you seem to be a bit more exasperated by him than he is of you."

She didn't like the tiny glimmer of hope that started in her chest. Duncan had stated quite bluntly that he couldn't love. Why she had no clue, but he obviously believed it, so she tried to darken the light. "We're just colleagues."

Holly snorted. "Yeah, and I'm the leaning Tower of Pisa. If you two are just colleagues then I'm sound asleep in my bed, dreaming all this up."

That little light in Jessica's chest burst back to life. "Remember, Duncan's a flirt. He's great at making women feel special."

"I don't know. I think you should reconsider your judgement. I didn't think Cam was seriously interested and yet look what happened with us." Holly looked away for a moment. "Do you think Cam will come see me again when we're done?"

Jessica hesitated. She didn't want to squash Holly's hope. "I'm not sure. He's kind of like my boss, so he keeps me on a need-to-know basis only." She gave Holly a half smile. She just wasn't sure that was such a good idea anyway, but she couldn't tell her that.

Movement on the couch distracted her. Cameron was in the process of pulling off the younger Holly's sweater. "Um, I think I'll go into another room."

Holly looked over at the couch and blushed, but she didn't follow Jessica as she floated into the tiny kitchen. It was one thing to spy on Holly's past, but she definitely wasn't about to become a voyeur. What was Cameron thinking sending them here at this time of night?

She stilled. It wasn't this time of night when she and Duncan had spoken outside. He'd pushed them further in time. She'd do the same thing right now if Holly wasn't so mesmerized by watching her old self with Cameron.

Why would Duncan have pushed them into this scene? Unless he was hoping it would get her in the mood. Seriously, the man seemed to have a one-track mind. Except the track he was on right now was to protect her.

She couldn't help but sigh over that. He really was concerned for her. He'd been worried about her at his castle too. Shit, the man had grown up in an actual castle. Life was very different at the turn of the nineteenth century. He had adapted well, though to be fair, he'd had over two hundred years to do so.

A moan from the other room derailed her thoughts. She couldn't imagine what it would be like to watch herself making love to a man she cared for. Just the thought of what she and Duncan must have looked like on the stairwell of his castle had her cheeks heating. Even then his instinct was to protect her from getting hurt.

What if he'd remembered they were dead and had continued with his lovemaking? Would he have taken her there on the stairs? She could have leaned forward and placed her hands on the higher steps. He was tall enough to easily throw up her skirt, nudge her legs apart and penetrate her.

Her folds moistened at the image of Duncan sliding into her from behind. He would at first sink slowly because he was the type of man who would savor the new experience of being inside her. He would lean over and grasp her breasts in his hands, his fingers finding her nipples and he'd play, refusing to move his hips.

She would be driven crazy by the lightning striking from her hardened nubs to her core. Her sheath would react, teasing him into moving.

He'd laugh at her attempt to make him lose control and instead he'd tease her back, leaving her nipples to let them brush against the stone step below her. Instead, he'd smooth his hands down her belly and into the hair between her legs. With expert skill he would find her clit with his finger and rub it down and up, slowly, building the fire within her.

Her juices would coat him and she'd moan, but he still wouldn't move. Desperate for release, she'd reach between her legs and cup his balls. He'd grab her wrist. "Ach, you're a sneaky one, lass."

She grinned as her imagination conjured Duncan at his best. Would he finally move? No, he wouldn't. But she would, and he'd grab her hips to still her, but she'd tighten and loosen her passage around him, anxious to feel him pump inside her.

His growl would fill her body as finally, he pulled out slowly only to glide back into her as far as he could go, his pelvis pressed hard against her ass, his cock pushing against her cervix. His hands would hold her tight against him as if he strove to gain control of his raging need. Then he'd pull out again, pushing back in faster this time.

Her nipples lightly brushed across the abrasive stone of the step as his hips met her ass. The fire at her core burned hot, the extra stimulation not needed, but welcome.

"Ach, lass, ye are a siren sent to whisk me away to the depth of the loch. I just know ye are."

She arched her back and pushed her ass more firmly against his pelvis.

A hiss issued from between his lips before he pulled back and rocked into her again.

Yes. This is what she wanted. The feel of his full cock sliding in and out of her, feeding the fire inside her. She closed her eyes, the sensations inside too intense.

Duncan's own need had finally conquered his control and his thrusts grew faster, his hands holding her hips, pulling her toward him as he rammed in and pushing her away as he pulled out. In and out, again and again, the fiery sensations flooding her like the tide coming in, wave after wave until they burst outward, engulfing her body with hot liquid pleasure.

She held on to the stone step as her world exploded. She yelled her gratification, her voice amplified by the stairway even as Duncan continued to pump into her, pushing her bliss to an intensity she'd never known.

The sound of Duncan's primal growl vibrated into her core just as he came inside her, flooding her sheath and sending her orgasm into another circle of ecstasy.

"Jessica?" Holly's voice penetrated her consciousness.

She opened her eyes and snapped her head toward the doorway, flushing with heat at being caught daydreaming.

"Are you okay?" Holly drifted closer.

"Yes, yes, just trying to figure out a problem Duncan and I were discussing earlier." She wiped the sweat off her palms against her skirt and pasted on a smile. "How are you doing?"

Holly tried to pull out a chair and her hand went through it instead. "Oh, I forgot." She grinned and folded her legs up under her to sit as she floated. "This is weird."

"I know, but it's only for one night."

Holly's brows drew together.

Jessica moved toward her and placed a hand on her shoulder. "What's wrong?"

She shrugged. "Nothing's wrong. You and Duncan have given me a lot to think about."

"In what way?"

Holly remained silent for a moment then she shrugged. "I'm not sure yet. My mind keeps going around in circles about Cam and me and you and me and you and Duncan."

"Me and Duncan? I thought we just determined there is no 'me and Duncan'. What would you have to think about us? We are just your Spirit Guides."

Holly raised her brow. "Oh, you're a lot more than that. He is totally mystified by you and you think he's a hunk. Not that I blame you, he is. So have you two had sex, or can you after you're dead?" Holly held up her hand. "No, don't tell me, I really don't want to know."

Jessica blushed, discounting Holly's assessment of her and

Duncan's relationship even as a flicker of yearning permeated her heart. He was her mentor, and yes, there were definitely sparks, but any woman spending any length of time with Duncan would spark off him. That was exactly why he was the way he was, and why she needed to keep him away from her heart…if it wasn't already too late. "Then what about you and Cameron? He chose these separate times in your past for a reason."

"Why does *he* get to choose?" Holly unfolded her legs and floated in a standing position.

She pointed up. "Because he's the boss."

"But what about what I want to see?"

Doubt niggled its way into her brain. That was a good question. As a case worker, she'd always been open to what the client thought would help him or her the most. If she agreed, it usually worked out better than foisting something onto them. But other case workers she'd known were adamant they knew best. Was this what she was facing now? "I know there is at least one other episode in your past that we will go to when Duncan gets back." Where was he? He could have popped back in minutes.

Holly crossed her arms. "I'm sure I'll love whatever time he chose because he chose it, but…"

She looked so sad, that Jessica couldn't stand it. "What is it? What time did you want to visit?"

Holly looked at her with tear-filled eyes. "If this is my only chance to revisit my past, I want to see the day Cameron proposed to me. It was the happiest day of my life, even more than the wedding because that day I finally understood our love for each other would last forever."

Jessica swallowed hard against the tears that threatened in her own eyes. It was so obvious that the love Cameron and Holly had was truly special, far exceeding most couples. Holly deserved to have her wish granted. What harm could it cause?

She turned away and tried to remember Duncan's training. Was there anything in the rules about adding another stop beyond what was prescribed? She pushed her glasses up to sit more firmly on her nose. If she'd had the itinerary from the start, she'd know if Holly's request was already covered. She so resented the "boys" keeping her out of the loop on her own case. This could serve them right.

She turned back to look at Holly and found her gazing at her with so much hope that there was no way she could turn down such a simple request. "I think we can do that."

"Really?" Holly's eyes lit with joy.

"Absolutely! This trip is about you. If it will make you happy then I'll take you."

Holly flew across the room and gave her a hug. Jessica wrapped her arms around the other woman and held her tight, a piece of her connecting with Holly, embracing her like the sister she never had. Finally, she laughed, her heart filled with happiness. "Shall we go?"

Holly smiled widely. "Yes. Oh wait, what about Duncan?"

What about him? Why wasn't he back? Was there a problem? "You're right. We should probably wait for him."

"Can't he find us?"

That was a question she couldn't answer. "I'm not sure." Her body tingled like it did when she phased through a solid Duncan. Maybe this wasn't the best idea. "I think he would be upset if he came back and found us missing. What time and place did Cameron propose to you?"

"We were hillwalking." Holly's face took on a look of pure bliss as she stared off into her memory. "It was less than a year after we met, but he always said, 'when you know it's right, you know'. It was a beautiful day. One of those days when you just feel like everything is right with the world. He hadn't even planned it, but that's so Cameron, always acting on the spur of the moment."

That surprised her. "He didn't plan it? So no ring?"

Holly shook her head. "Nope. It was spontaneous, like it burst out from his soul."

The dreamy look on the younger woman had Jessica yearning for something else, but her time had passed. The elaborate proposal in the five-star restaurant in Portland had been all the show and surprise a woman could ask for. Jacob said all the right things, everything said in every romantic movie she'd ever seen. He'd probably studied those movies and bought the two-carat diamond ring to be sure she would say yes. And she had. She fell for it hook, line and sinker.

She looked down at her hand, the engagement ring wasn't there. She tried to remember if she'd even noticed it was missing since she'd been in the afterlife. How odd. Did that mean she wasn't buried with it? She reached up to her ears. She had her earrings, even her jewelry box back at the cottage.

"How long do we need to wait?" Holly interrupted her thoughts. "I only have tonight, right?"

Jessica pushed her glasses up the bridge of her nose. She wasn't sure what to do. Part of her said to do whatever it took to make Holly happy, but a part of her was very aware she hadn't paid the attention to Duncan's training she should have. It was his fault for being Mr. Distraction.

Then again, she knew the number-one rule, which was to stay phased, so she should be able to handle anything else.

"Come." She held her hand out to Holly, ignoring the tingle that ran through her again. She was probably just excited. "Let's go visit that little hill where Cameron proposed to you before he'd even known you for a year."

Holly grabbed her hand with enthusiasm.

Her heart filled, reassuring her she did the right thing. "Ready?"

"Ready."

She floated them out of the Victorian and toward Scotland.

~*~

Duncan threw open the door of Cameron's office, no' caring that his assistant said he had someone with him. "Cameron, what the blazes is going on?"

The man in the chair in front of Cameron's desk rose. "Hey, if you don't mind, we were having an important conversation here."

Duncan glanced at the man, taking in his youth, bulky build and shaved head. "Get out."

The young man's eyes slitted, giving Duncan plenty of warning. As the fist came his way, he grabbed it and pulled, throwing the man across the room to hit the wall hard. Guess he hadn't passed the phase training yet.

"Duncan, that's enough."

He returned his attention to Cameron. "I haven't even started. You need to answer some questions and answer them now before Jessica becomes a lost soul."

Cameron's brow lowered. "I have no idea what you're talking about."

Duncan started around the desk, but the young man he'd thrown didn't seem to understand he wasn't wanted. He charged.

Duncan took part of a second to completely phase and watch the new recruit slam headlong into Cameron's desk. He fell to the floor, unmoving. "No' very smart."

"Neither are you." Cameron eyes were hard as flint.

"It's hard to be smart when my friend is hiding information from me. Tell me why every event you have us visiting with Holly is revealing hard-to-swallow truths to Jessica. I can see the doubt in her eyes. Her life is unraveling before her and her acceptance of being dead is leaving." He tried to control his anger, but the look in Jessica's face when she connected her suggestion to Tommy and the foregoing meeting of Holly and Cameron was the last straw.

Cameron looked away. "That's why you're there. You're her mentor, so mentor her."

Duncan shook his head. "Ach, you dinna get away with laying this on me. You chose those episodes in Holly's life for a reason and the reason had nothing to do with Holly."

Cameron stood silent, unmoving.

"Blast it, man, what have ye done? Is this assignment even approved?"

Cameron finally faced him. "Yes, it's approved." He came out from behind his desk and pointed at him. "It's your job to keep Jessica in line and Holly safe."

Duncan smacked Cameron's hand aside. "I'll be happy to do that when you give me all the information about this case. Every episode has a tie to Jessica. You knew that and used it to make Holly comfortable on the first visit to her past, but now you are crossing a line."

Cameron's eyebrow rose. "Really? And what line would that be? I have a new Spirit Guide who thinks she knows everything and an old Spirit Guide trainer who hasn't used his brain or his heart to solve a client problem in two hundred years! As far as I'm concerned, just talking to you is cutting you slack."

Relief washed through Duncan. "So this is about me. Fine, but leave the lass out of it."

Cameron laughed. "Oh that's perfect. Now it's all about you. Hate to tell you, it's about getting the job done that you and Jessica were sent to do, which was to bring my wife to a level of happiness she has not been at since I died. It's really not that hard to do. If you mess up with Jessica and she screws up, then so be it. You just make sure Holly is in a better place when you're done."

Duncan's gut twisted. He couldn't just take the case away from Jessica. She'd be devastated if she didn't help Holly. Cameron was always concerned about his Spirit Guides finding confidence. This assignment was undermining everything Jessica believed. Duncan wouldn't let that happen.

He'd never seen Cameron like this. The man's usual calm manner had completely disappeared. What happened to the man he'd had drinks with and laughed over his past mistakes with? The Cameron he faced now was someone else entirely. There was no way Duncan would sacrifice Jessica for Cameron's wife, bugger the rules. Besides, Cameron could always take care of his wife. Obviously, no one gave three figs for Jessica.

Duncan forced his fisted hands to remain at his sides. "Fine. Then I'll bring Jessica back and finish the assignment by myself."

"That's not an option." Cameron looked him in the eyes. "If you have to hump the woman to focus, then do it and get it over with. Then get back to Holly."

The entire room turned red and Duncan lunged for Cameron. He wrapped his hands around the man's neck and squeezed. No one spoke about Jessica that way. She was everything good at heart, trying as hard as she could to help other people and this man kept throwing her life back in her face.

Cameron's hands pried at his fingers, but he wouldn't let go. Duncan's rage found release in hurting the man who caused Jessica pain and heartache. He wanted him dead. Huh? He watched as Cameron's eyes rolled back. But they all were dead already.

"Duncan. Duncan!"

He blinked. Cameron had his hand on his arm, his brow furrowed with concern. Duncan stared at his neck, no marks marred it.

Then a sharp pain seeped into his brain, filling it from the bottom up. He grabbed his head. "Argh." There was no pain in the afterlife. What was happening?

Cameron grabbed him by both shoulders and force-phased him.

The pain eased, only a shadow of what it was, though it still remained in a ball at the base of his head. He looked into Cameron's concerned gaze. "What was that?"

"It's what I feared. You need to finish this assignment sooner rather than later. Only then can I help you."

"Help me? What do you mean?"

Cameron floated away and solidified. "I know what's causing these episodes, but you have to finish this assignment with Jessica before we can address it."

"Why can't we address it now?"

Cameron strode back to his desk. "Because how far gone you are will depend upon the outcome of this case."

How far gone? What did that mean? He opened his mouth to ask when something inside him shuddered at what the answer would be. Instead, he tried one more time to get some answers for Jessica if no' for himself.

Cameron studied him. "Have you been having many of these episodes?"

Had he? He'd had the one when he thought he was making love to Jessica. Before that he'd had one when he'd finally won a bet on the Rangers game against Cameron for the first time. It had been sweet triumph until the pain started. He shrugged. "A few."

Cameron turned away to walk back behind his desk. "Then I suggest you get back to work."

"Can you no' tell me anything about this link between Holly and Jessica?" He hated asking when he wanted to demand the information, but it was clear that wasn't going to work, especially as he had to remain phased and couldn't beat it out of Cameron.

His boss shrugged. "Just focus on Holly and the rest will work itself out."

Duncan drifted to the front of the desk, he wanted to solidify, but the vestiges of the head pain still hung at the base of his neck. "There's more to this case than just your wife. Can you no' see that?"

Cameron's eyes remained cold. "There's more to this case than just Jessica. Why can't *you* see that?"

Duncan swallowed. He'd never felt the way he did now and he wasn't even sure what it was he felt. All he knew was he would do anything to protect Jessica from hurt of any kind be it emotional, physical or mental.

His anger lessened at that realization, but he dared no' delve into the why and wherefore of it. "But you do admit there is more to this assignment than simply helping your wife?"

Cameron held his gaze for a good minute before he gave the slightest nod.

A moan from the floor had Duncan looking beneath him. The young Spirit Guide was coming to. He could either knock him out again or leave.

Obviously, he wouldn't get any more answers from Cameron now. He needed to get back to Jessica for whatever else she would be forced to face.

Giving his friend a final glare, he floated through the floor and toward Holly's apartment. He flew through time and space much faster than when he had Holly and Jessica with him. As he traveled, he thought to switch his clothing, but the pain at the base of his skull grew stronger, so he stopped and it went back to a dull ache. Guess he'd stay in the tight clothes of the present a little longer.

He'd hoped to surprise Jessica with his native wear, something to take her mind off her doubts. He'd just have to use something else to distract her.

He grinned as he floated into the little apartment to find the young Holly and Cameron asleep on the couch. He'd forgotten to go back to the time he'd left the women, but that was fine. They weren't there so they had to be in the kitchen. The apartment wasn't that big.

When he didn't find them there, he moved into the bedroom.

He stared at the empty room in disbelief. Where could they have gone? Outside?

He'd just go back to when he left them. He floated back to the kitchen, going back in time as he did and found them talking. He grinned. "Did you miss me, ladies?"

Holly smiled widely. "Yes. Oh wait, what about Duncan?"

He floated forward. "What about me?"

Jessica frowned. "You're right. We should probably wait for him."

"I'm right here." What the blazes was happening? "Jessica. You can see me, lass?"

"Can't he find us?" Holly looked right past him.

"I'm not sure."

He phased through Jessica, the pain in his head spiking again. Blast. Surely she could feel that.

"I think he would be upset if he came back and found us missing. What time and place did Cameron propose to you?"

Duncan shook his head "Missing, why would I find you missing? What does it matter when he proposed to her? No. Jessica."

"We were hillwalking." Holly's face softened. "It was less than a year after we met, but he always said, 'when you know it's right, you know'. It was a beautiful day. One of those days when you just feel like everything is right with the world. He hadn't even planned it, but that's so Cameron, always acting on the spur of the moment."

"He didn't plan it? So no ring?"

Holly shook her head. "Nope. It was spontaneous, like it burst out from his soul."

Jessica looked down at her hand.

Duncan tried to take that hand, but there was no connection.

"How long do we need to wait?" Holly's impatience was clear. "I only have tonight, right?"

Jessica pushed her glasses up the bridge of her nose. "Come." She held her hand out to Holly.

Fear sliced through him. "Blast it, Jessica, do no' do—argh." He grasped his head in his hands at the pain.

Jessica smiled. "Let's go visit that little hill where Cameron proposed to you."

Holly grabbed her hand.

"Ready?"

"Ready."

"No!" Duncan threw himself at Jessica, but she floated away.

Chapter Seven

Jessica held on to Holly's hand tight. Without Duncan along, Holly's well-being was in her hands. This was a good test for her. Still, she couldn't shake the feeling Duncan wouldn't be happy, but the fact was, Holly would be and that's what counted.

As the dark of time dissipated, she guided them over the coast that lined the verdant land of Scotland. The view reminded her of Duncan's castle and a need to know if it was still there during her lifetime grew.

She glanced at Holly to see anticipation written in her half smile. Maybe after they watched Cameron propose, they could look for it together.

She flew them south of the River Clyde for a bit before turning eastward toward the hill. As they drew closer, it was obvious why it was called Loudon Hill. It had an inviting rounded top and green landscape with trees encircling part of it. Compared to the flat fields surrounding it, which were dotted with sheep, it looked as high as some of the small mountains in New Hampshire she'd hiked. One side was a cliff, but most of it looked like an easy hike through grass.

Holly pointed. "See that rock face?"

Jessica nodded. It would be hard not to see it.

"Cam loved to climb that on the weekends when he had no bigger challenges scheduled. He said it kept him in shape. But I swear he knew where every crack and crevice was on that thing. You'd think he was Spider-Man. But on the day he proposed we took the long way up for my benefit."

As they floated over the top of the hill, Holly squealed, "There."

From above, Jessica could see what looked to be a small monolith at the very top, probably a monument to somebody historical, surrounded by a grassy area. Not far from the very top was a tree, slightly leaning, its heavy branches providing welcome shade on the sunny day for the couple beneath it.

All their scheduled visits had been at night. She hoped she wasn't breaking some spirit rule. She looked at Holly again as they drew close and her anxious face was enough for Jessica. Rules, shmules, Holly needed this.

They came to a stop just feet away from the shade. The young Holly leaned against the trunk of the tree while Cameron lay with his head in her lap. Both wore shorts and t-shirts and two walking sticks were on the ground nearby.

Holly released her hand and floated closer to the couple before looking up at Jessica. "Oh, this is perfect timing."

She drifted a bit closer as well, her excitement at seeing the proposal heightening.

Cameron picked a nearby mayweed flower from the ground. "Come here."

Holly grinned. "I am here."

"No, lass. Bend down and give me a kiss."

The young Holly pretended to ponder his request before she lowered her lips to his. Jessica watched as Cameron held the young woman's head with one hand and slipped the tiny flower behind her ear with the other.

Young Holly lifted her head. "You taste like chocolate. Did you bring chocolate with you?"

He shrugged. "I may have, but you said you were on a diet."

She rolled her eyes. "Really Cam? You know I'm always on a diet and I'm always ignoring it. You're going to have to share that chocolate."

"Be happy to. All you have to do is give me another kiss."

He winked at her and she laughed. "You are such a tease."

He grinned. "I try." He reached out and picked another mayweed flower. He plucked one white petal off it. "She loves me."

"Oh, don't break the flower."

He looked fondly up at her. "It's okay, I put one in your hair to help keep its beauty, but now that I look at it, it doesn't come close to yours."

The young Holly blushed. "You shouldn't say that. I'll start believing you and then my head will be too big to fit into the door of our apartment."

"Don't worry. If your head gets too big, we'll just find a flat with a big enough door."

Holly chuckled. "You have an answer for everything."

"Aye." He lay there gazing into her eyes.

Jessica's throat closed at the emotion flowing between the young couple. She looked over at Holly and found the same look on her face. An old ache, like the one she had before she met Jacob, grew in her chest. She thought she'd found the one, but even if she'd never known Jacob had been unfaithful, seeing Holly and Cameron would have made it clear, she would never know love at the depth they had or the depth she had always wanted.

Cameron's hand with the flower rose and she watched as he picked off every petal as he spoke. "She loves me. She loves me. She loves me. She loves me!"

Holly laughed. "That's not how it goes."

Cameron jumped up and pulled her up. "It does for me."

She nodded even as her laughter continued. "Yes, you're right. I love everything about you."

Cameron sobered. "Holly love, be my wife. I love you more than there are stars, higher than this wee hill, and longer than life. Please, say yes."

The young Holly's stunned expression had Jessica swallowing hard against the tears of joy that threatened.

Then Holly's face changed. Her eyes teared up and her lips lifted into a breathtaking smile. "Yes."

Cameron scooped her into a bear hug before lifting her feet off the ground and twirling her around.

Holly squealed.

Jessica's gaze locked with the older Holly's.

"See why I wanted to come?"

Jessica nodded, her throat too tight to speak.

Cameron finally slowed and took young Holly's face between his hands. "I swear I will love you forever and strive to make you as happy as you've made me for the rest of my life."

"And I swear I will love you forever and make sure you do exactly as you said."

Cameron threw his head back and laughed. "You, my hen, are one of a kind."

"So are you."

Cameron lifted his head and yelled. "She said yes!"

"Cam."

He looked down at her, love making his eyes look like gem stones. "What? I want the world to know you will be my wife."

Holly grinned. "But there is no one for miles around. Besides, if you want to do that, you better get me an engagement ring pretty quick."

His surprised look made it clear he'd completely forgotten he needed to do that. He released Holly so fast she lost her balance, but she caught herself as he ran to a nearby bush.

"Cam, what are you doing?"

"Just stay right there."

The young Holly folded her arms and shook her head.

Jessica glanced at the older Holly. "What is he doing?"

"Just watch. I still love it."

"Och. What the hell?" Cameron backed away from the bush then lay on the ground and peered under it.

"Are you okay?" Young Holly looked puzzled, but not concerned.

"Yeah, I'm fine, stay there."

Jessica watched from where she was, though the urge to float over to the bush was strong, but Holly wanted her to be surprised so she made herself stay where she was.

"Okay, close your eyes and hold out your hands." Cameron looked over his shoulder at Holly.

"Really, Cam?"

"Come on, love, just do it."

Young Holly closed her eyes and held out her arms.

Cameron finally rose and carried something in his hands, but from where she drifted, she could see a tiny tail sticking out. Oh, she hoped it wasn't a rodent. Would he play that kind of trick on the woman who just agreed to marry him?

"I've brought you an engagement gift." Cameron placed the animal in Holly's hands.

The second she felt it, she opened her eyes. "What? Where?" She held a tiny furball of kitten.

"It's Mac." Jessica couldn't help her surprise.

The older Holly nodded. "Yup. He found him under that bush when he went to break off a twig."

"Why did he need a twig?"

"You'll see." Holly grinned with undisguised glee. She really was enjoying this.

Young Holly tried to cuddle the kitten, but it kept climbing onto her shoulder and licking her ear. She giggled and pulled it down again. "He's as bad as you only a lot smaller."

Cameron grinned. "He's one smart cat. He knew exactly where to hide so I could find him."

Holly scanned the area. "But where's his mom and siblings? He's too young to be at the top of Loudon Hill by himself."

Cameron scratched the top of the kitten's head and he started to purr. "We'll look for them as we head down, but if we don't find them, you'll have to keep him."

Holly nodded solemnly and pulled the kitten from her shoulder again.

"Before we head down, I want you to wear this." Cameron took young Holly's left hand and placed a twig ring on her finger.

She started to cry in earnest. "Oh Cam."

He pulled her into his embrace and kissed her. The kitten pounced onto his shoulder and bit his ear. "Ow. Stop that." The kitten hesitated then licked his ear.

Young Holly laughed. "If we get to keep him I'm going to call him Mac. He's so much like you."

Cameron's eyes widened. "What does Mac have to do with me? I'm a Douglas."

"Cam spelled backwards is Mac." The twinkle in her eye was reflected in his and he laughed.

"Your brain works in crazy ways, hen, but I love it."

Young Holly gave him a quick kiss on the cheek. "I know it does. Now let's see if we can find Mac's family. No one should be without family."

Cameron gave her ass a squeeze as she bent to retrieve their walking sticks. "Cam, stop."

He wiggled his eyebrows as he took his stick from her. "I'm thinking we can make our own family."

Young Holly blushed, but Jessica noticed the older Holly was anything but happy. A tear made its way slowly down her cheek.

Jessica floated over to her. "What's wrong?"

She shook her head. "Nothing."

"'Nothing' doesn't cause people to cry. You were so happy a moment ago. Tell me."

Holly sniffed as she wiped her eyes with her sleeve. "We had planned on trying for a baby right away, but then Cameron came up with the idea of the One of A Kind Christmas Shop and we decided to wait. If we hadn't waited, I would have a piece of him with me now."

"But you do have a piece of him. Actually, you have all of him. Cameron still loves you and you still love him. In fact, he loves you so much, he sent me and Duncan here to make you happy. It's not about what might have been, but about what you have had."

Jessica paused. Holly didn't seem to understand her point.

"What you had with Cameron, that's something only one in a million people have. It's to be treasured and respected for its beauty as it was, not for what it could have led to."

Holly sniffed again. "I think I see what you're saying. By wishing for more, I'm kind of putting down what we *did* have, like it wasn't good enough."

"Exactly."

"I think I need a hug."

Jessica smiled and wrapped her arms around the woman. She so wanted Holly to be happy. So much so that if she had the chance to bring back Cameron from the dead she would. Since that wasn't an option, she'd have to make do with hugs and counsel. She just hoped it was enough.

Duncan floated into Jessica's cottage, his heart racing with fear. Jessica was in danger. No' only had she strayed from the pre-planned itinerary, but she'd done it for Holly. The connection between the two women was growing too strong. As soon as he found her, he'd warn her…that is if he could.

He looked at his hands. They were still wavy and unclear. He hadn't even noticed that until he'd been left alone in Holly's home. His phased state wasn't normal. It could be because Cameron had force-phased him instead of him phasing himself, but he couldn't solidify among the living.

He floated to the neat desk at one end of Jessica's living room. Relief that Holly's file was in plain sight washed through him. He solidified, reaching his hand toward the file, but caught the back of the desk chair as searing pain struck through his head and down his back, sending him to his knees. "Argh!"

He took deep breaths, refusing the comfort of his phased state. He couldn't pick up the file in that state. The pain was excruciating, like a sword driving through the top of his skull. Think of Jessica. She needed him. Jessica, with the cute nose and bonnie green eyes a man could lose himself in. Her laughter and smiles and warm, caring heart. She needed him.

The pain lessened as he focused on her. He wouldn't let anything happen to her. She was worth ten of him. He didn't want her doubting herself or her life. She'd done so much good while alive. He wanted her to succeed. He wanted her to understand that he would take care of her.

Why?

The pain began to ease. She was important to him. He cared about her. He liked her. They could have a lasting afterlife together.

He stilled. That wasn't something he'd ever thought about before. Why now? He shied away from delving into it. He had a woman to save.

Standing slowly, he kept his head completely level. When no

stabbing agony rocked his skull, he moved it left and right, then up and down. The pain had disappeared. Finally, he could get back to Jessica.

He grabbed the file and rifled through it until he found what he needed, the day Cameron proposed. Immediately, he phased and inspected his hands. The wavy appearance was gone. Hopefully, that meant he'd be able to communicate with Jessica again.

That Cameron knew what was wrong with him but wouldn't tell him until after their assignment had him thinking far less of the man. Either he was completely selfish about his wife being the priority at all costs, or he didn't think he could help Duncan unless he finished this assignment. Either way, his gut told him, he wouldn't like the explanation.

The whispers about spirits disappearing floated through his mind again. There weren't many trainers or Spirit Guides who had been dead as long as him. He tried to think of those who were and couldn't. It didn't matter at the moment anyway. Jessica was his priority just as Holly was Cameron's.

Duncan sped across space and time. As he flew over the place where his castle once stood, his heart sank. One lone tower and a piece of the castle wall stood like silent sentinels of his family's line. The Montgomeries had carried on without him, probably thanks to his older brother, up until the last assignment he'd had this way, but to see his home all but gone was a blow to his heart. Had they scattered to the four winds?

Loudon Hill came into view. He moved even faster toward the spot, hoping he wasn't too late to stop the growing connection between Jessica and Holly. Two individuals walked across the top of the large hill in the middle of fields. Beneath a tree near the top, he could see the two women.

Quickly, he landed before them.

"Duncan." Jessica's welcoming smile was like a balm to his soul, but he didn't let his comfort at her ability to see him cloud his concern.

"What have ye done, lass?"

Her smile disappeared. "I brought Holly to the place where Cameron proposed. It's what she wanted."

Holly floated next to Jessica. "It's true. This is my only chance to relive my moments with Cameron and I wanted to see this."

He turned toward Holly. "I understand, lass, I do, but we have rules and this visit could have serious repercussions."

"I'm sorry. I didn't mean to cause any harm. I just wanted to see more of Cameron."

He set his hand on her shoulder and forced a smile. "I know. How about you float down the hill with him while I talk to Jessica. We'll meet you down there."

Holly nodded. "I can do that. Just remember, it was my idea." She gave him a stern look before she floated after Cameron.

He didn't say anything until Holly had disappeared over the crest of the hill. Then he faced Jessica.

She pushed her glasses up as if readying for battle. On one hand, he admired her for that, but on the other, his fear for her built. "Take my hand."

Thankful she didn't balk or try to argue, he clasped her hand tightly and headed for his castle in the afterlife. He hadn't gone far when her hand slipped from his.

"Jessica?" He looked back but she wasn't there. His heart thudded to a stop before his brain overrode his shock and he sped back to Loudon Hill.

She floated on the opposite side from where Holly had gone. "What happened?"

He pulled at the neckline of the tight shirt he wore, no' willing to believe he was too late. "You let go of my hand."

"No, I didn't. I was pulled away from you like a sling shot and came to a stop right here."

Bollocks! He was too late. He couldn't accept it, wouldn't accept it.

"Duncan, what's wrong? You're scaring me." Jessica's eyes were wide, her body tense.

He tried to loosen his scowl, but a pain had started in his chest that was completely different from the pain he'd been getting in his head. This one made him want to die all over again. "It is your connection to Holly."

"What do you mean?"

He grabbed her by the shoulders, relieved he still could. "You're connection to Holly has grown too strong. It won't allow you to leave the plane of the living."

"Do you mean I can't go back to my job as Spirit Guide or my little cottage or even to your castle?" Her voice rose in pitch.

The image of the castle as it stood now raced through his mind to be replaced by an image of Jessica, sprawled across the bed in his tower room, waiting for him to join her. He shook his head to clear it, no' anxious to have more of the head pain he'd had before. "No you can't, but only for now." He looked away, no' wanting her to see he had no idea if there was anything he could do to save her.

She leaned against him, wrapping her arms around his waist. "Oh good. You scared me. She lifted her head. When can I go back?"

He couldn't look at the trust in her eyes and lie, so he rested his hand against her head and nudged her face to his chest. "I dinna know yet. I need to consult with Cameron." There had to be a way to save her from becoming a ghost. That he could hold her meant she wasn't completely gone. There had to be something they could do.

He pulled back to look at her. *I can't lose her.* "First you need to break the connection with Holly as much as possible."

She pulled out of his arms. "How am I supposed to do that?"

"You can't give in to her. You can counsel her and support her, but you have to detach yourself from her."

"And if I don't?"

Then there's no hope for us. He didn't even understand he wanted an "us" until just minutes earlier, or were there any minutes? Frustration built at the situation Cameron had caused. "If you dinna, then you will never get back to the afterlife."

Her face paled and her voice came out in a whisper. "Never?"

"I promise, I will do everything I can to get you back, but you have to disconnect emotionally."

Jessica's fear was palpable. "I don't know how to do that. I never could while I was alive." Tears welled in her eyes. "Oh no, I'm going to be a ghost aren't I?"

He grabbed her to him and held her tight. "Nay. I won't let that happen."

She clung to him and his heart constricted. When had she come to mean everything to him? How could this happen? And what the blazes could he do about it?

Jessica lifted her face from his shoulder and gazed at him, her fear so stark, his own spiked. "Ach, lass. You're a confident, capable woman. You've made miracles happen for others. You can make one happen for yourself. Remember, Holly will have two more ghosts to help her. Just as the Tinders took over with Holly, and Mrs. Connors was helped by the people at Willow Wood. You've already done so much for her, but now you can let her go."

Jessica looked away. "Will I get to see how her life goes after the other spirits visit her?"

He brushed a loose strand of silky blonde hair away from her face. "Aye. But only if you disconnect. You must be a Spirit Guide to see how everything works out for her. If you stay connected, you will be stuck here even after she dies."

She moved her hand toward her glasses and he caught it. "Jess, no more self-doubt. I've never met a more capable, beautiful or intelligent woman with such a big heart. You must find the will to separate."

He held her gaze, wanting more than anything to give her his own will, but he couldn't.

"You really believe that?" Her vulnerability almost broke his heart. How could she think otherwise?

"Every word of it." He didn't smile. He needed her to know how much he thought of her.

Her hand in his moved to his cheek. Then she rose on her toes and kissed him. Her tongue provocatively traced his lips before urging him to open them.

He acquiesced and allowed her to take the lead, hoping with all his heart he wasn't in another "zombie" state.

Her arms wrapped around his neck and she pressed her breasts into him. As her tongue grew more demanding, he tightened his hold and met her with a taste of his own passion.

Her hands fisted against his neck and a small moan from deep inside her reverberated inside his mouth. Suddenly, she pulled her lips away. "Make love to me, Duncan."

Her words were the sweetest he'd ever heard in his entire existence. He couldn't deny her if he wanted to, and he definitely didn't want to. "Ach, Jess." He pulled her mouth back to his and swept his tongue inside, intensifying what she'd started. He didn't care that it wasn't where and how he'd planned when he'd first met her. All he knew was he needed to connect with her, keep her with him, make her his.

He held her flush against him, her taste spurring his need even as her tart scent surrounded him like a warm cocoon. Her soft body melded to his, making him want to dive inside her, but she was far too precious for that. She needed to be unwrapped, like a special gift.

Jessica lifted the back of his t-shirt and burrowed her fingers beneath the waistband of his jeans.

His cock jumped as she moved one hand downward and grasped his ass.

He pulled his mouth from hers. "Lass, if ye dinna want to find yourself on your back in three seconds then ye'd best remove your hand from my arse."

She shook her head. "No. I want to feel you everywhere. I want to touch all this raw muscle I've been daydreaming about." Her eyes started to water. "I want to know one more moment of sheer pleasure in case I never can again."

"Jess, I dinna'—"

Her finger on his lips silenced him. "No. We don't know for sure. Let me pretend you care. Let me have this one slice of heaven."

Blast. He did care, so much. His gut twisted at the thought that her last wish could be to lay with him. That this meant heaven to her, humbled him. He nodded against her finger.

"Good. Then get undressed."

He widened his eyes, about to tell her they should take it slow, but she'd pulled her blouse over her head and dropped it on the ground. Her full breasts pushed against her bra, begging for release. He would be happy to release them.

"Duncan." She moved toward him and pulled his t-shirt up.

"Aye, I can do it." Her touch was sending fire to his cock. He reached behind him and pulled the shirt over his head.

"Oh wow." She stared at him, her mouth open and her gaze fixed on his chest. Proudly, he remained still, beyond pleased she found him to her liking.

Chapter Eight

Jessica tried to close her mouth, but her brain just wouldn't function. Duncan Montgomerie would no longer be Mr. Distraction. He'd just graduated to Mr. Obsession. No man she'd ever met had such a hard physique. No wonder the sleeves of his t-shirt were stretched to their limits. The man's biceps were huge with those sexy veins running across them in all the right places, like his own skin could barely contain all that muscle. His pectorals were built, making his rounded chest appear too large for his slender waist. The six-pack of his abdominals was almost an eight-pack. And those developed Vs heading under his waistband had her drooling.

Oh gosh, she *was* drooling. She licked her lips to hide her reaction. He hovered there, letting her look, watching her. There was pride in his eyes, which he had a right to feel, but something else. Uncertainty?

That was crazy. What woman wouldn't want him?

She cooled. What woman hadn't had him was the better question. She should float away right now, but to what? She had nothing, and her future was too bleak to contemplate. This may be her last chance. Screw it. She didn't care if she was half in love with him and he only saw her as a mentee. He agreed when she asked and she would take all he had to offer. If her heart was broken later, what did it matter if she was doomed to haunt the living as a ghost anyway?

She shuddered and Duncan's brows lowered with concern. He really was sweet. "Are you going to take off your pants or do I need to help you?" Without shoes on, it wouldn't be hard to do.

His eyes widened and a crooked grin quirked up his lips.

That's the Duncan she wanted. The seducer. She needed him to make her forget, just for a brief time, what might await her.

He slowly undid his button and unzipped his zipper.

She pushed her skirt down and let it puddle on the ground as she floated up and out of it. When she looked at Duncan again he stood naked. Her blood heated. Even the light breeze buffeting the hilltop did nothing to cool her off.

Duncan's thighs were full of muscle, which made a great backdrop to his rigid cock. She flushed, thrilled that he wanted her.

"Lass, did ye need help undressing?"

Duh, here she hung, gawking at him instead of stripping. It was strange to be on top of a hill in Scotland getting naked. At least none of the living were around. "Wait, what about Holly?"

He shook his head. "Jess, we both know, Holly will no' leave Cameron's side for an instant."

"You're right." Relieved by the truth of his words, she reached behind her and unhooked her bra, then let it fall forward. She watched Duncan's face and a titillating spark jolted through her body at the hunger in his eyes. Then, as gracefully as she could, she pulled down her slip and floated out of it.

Duncan's face didn't change and she wondered if he'd gone zombie on her again, but then his chest rose and he let out a heavy breath. Did that mean he liked what he saw?

Lastly, she stepped out of her panties and stood facing him, as naked as the day she was born.

Air whistled through his teeth. "Ach, ye are even more bonnie than my imaginings."

His gaze was so intent and honest as it roamed over her, that it reminded her of all the lovely things he'd said about her earlier. That's what had her asking him to make love to her. That and her uncertain future. She swallowed her emotions before speaking. "You imagined me?"

He floated toward her, his grin devilish. "Aye, many times. Would ye like me to tell ye how I envisioned myself inside of ye?"

She sucked in her breath. When Duncan turned on the charm, he made her feel like a candle thrown in a fireplace. If she'd been standing, her knees would have buckled. She licked her lips. "No, I would prefer you showed me." Her voice came out almost desperate.

His grin faded as he took her face in both his hands. "It would be my pleasure." He searched her eyes like he was looking for an answer to something that troubled him. "I promise it will be your pleasure too." His seductive grin was back and she released the breath she didn't realize she'd held.

Duncan pulled her glasses from her face. "Your eyes are too entrancing to be hidden behind these."

"They are practical. This way I can see far away."

He walked behind her head and played with the barrette that held her hair back. "Ye dinna need to see anything at all. Just feel."

Oh, she felt all right. She felt hot and achy and needy, but she did want to see him, all of him.

His pine scent wafted around her and she breathed in. She loved his aroma. He managed to figure out her clip, and loosened her hair, its silky texture soft against her bare shoulders. His hands ran through it as if discovering hair for the first time. She heard him inhale then his exhale brushed the skin at the back of her neck and she trembled with wanting.

He finally drifted in front of her again. Just looking at him had her body humming.

Duncan pressed his lips to hers in the gentlest of kisses, not pushing, just tasting as if he were paying homage to some great Celtic priestess of old. She wrapped her arms around his waist and melded her body to his. At the touch of phased skin to phased skin, she sighed into his mouth. Every inch of her body where they touched buzzed with warmth and pleasure.

At her move, Duncan's hands on her head tightened, the only sign he felt what she felt, except for his hard cock pressing into her abdomen more firmly.

He cocked her head to kiss her jaw and then the spot beneath her ear that tickled. Unable to help herself, she lifted her shoulder to her ear, and he pulled his head away.

"Ye dinna like to be kissed there?" He looked so surprised she barely held in a giggle.

"I'm ticklish there."

He raised one eyebrow. "Good to know."

The very modern expression coming from him struck her as funny and she did chuckle.

Duncan wrapped his arms around her and squeezed. "Ach, Jess, ye make me happy."

She grinned against his shoulder. "That's not saying much. You're always that way. Forever smiling and grinning and smirking and—"

He pulled back to look at her. "Aye, but ye make me deep down happy."

Her heart took notice of his serious expression. "I'm glad." They stared at each other, the moment too important for words. Then he pulled her tight against him again.

"Ye feel so good."

She agreed, but didn't think he needed to know. The man had to realize he was a chick magnet.

His hands stroked her back as if he was interested in every inch of her. She did the same to him, though she couldn't reach half of it. The man had seriously broad shoulders.

When his hands found her butt cheeks and squeezed, her sheath moistened. Reactively, she tried to squeeze his hard ass, but she only succeeded in pressing herself tighter against him.

She felt his silent chuckle against her breasts, already sensitized by his rock-hard chest. He lowered his head to kiss her shoulder, staying far away from her ticklish spot.

She gave up on squeezing and simply enjoyed running her hands over his taut butt.

When Duncan's hands grasped her waist and pushed her upward, she let go of his ass and grabbed his shoulders. His lips traveled across her collarbone to the base of her throat. She swallowed as his tongue licked at the tiny hollow there.

"You taste like honey."

His words flowed through her even as he positioned her higher. His lips traveled down to the spot between her breasts and his tongue licked the sides of each. Shit, the man was such a tease. Her nipples were hard with anticipation, her folds swelling in preparation.

Duncan licked the underside of one breast, stopping to suck the full roundness. She tried to move downward, her nipples aching to be touched, but his grip was firm on her waist, his gentle strength far too much for her to challenge.

Even as that thought registered, her body tingled. He was in charge of her pleasure. She doubted she could find herself in better hands.

Duncan continued his licking and sucking, even pushing his large nose under her breast to nudge it up so he could kiss her there. When he lowered her, she silently sighed with relief.

But Duncan simply continued his travels around her breast, kissing his way to her areola, licking around her painfully hard nubs. "Please, Duncan."

He pulled back and looked at her. "Please what? What would you like of me?"

Her throat closed. Did she really want to tell him what to do and when to do it? No. He had plenty of experience and she would bet money he knew more about what would make her toes curl than she did. The idea of giving up control completely to him made her limbs flood with heat. "It feels so good. I need more."

He grinned, his look promising more than she anticipated and her stomach flipped.

"Aye, and that you'll have." When he lowered his head again, he immediately latched on to her right nipple and sucked.

She grabbed his head as tingles raced through every part of her body, her sheath tightening. Then his teeth caught her rock-hard nub and his tongue flicked against it. Sizzling pleasure shot from her breast to her core. She moaned.

Duncan pulled his head back, his teeth firmly locked around her nipple as he looked up at her. She closed her eyes, her folds filling with her juices, her body primed for him.

He opened his mouth and let go before licking the sensitive nub and sucking it hard.

Instinctively, she wrapped her legs around his waist, her need building fast.

But Duncan didn't seem to be in any hurry. He moved his attention to her left breast and started over, gently sucking her nipple, then taking it between his teeth and teasing it, before pulling at it and letting go, only to lave it again and suck it hard.

Her hips moved of their own accord. Duncan's cock head teasing her ass as she was too high to spear herself on it.

Then Duncan moved her higher. His lips tracing down her stomach, leaving kisses and nips on her hips, across her abdomen. Oh, wow, he was headed for the juncture of her thighs. She unclasped her legs from around his body, floating freely in the place he wanted her.

His hands on her waist moved to her hips as he positioned

her higher and pressed a kiss against the tiny spot of blonde hair on her mons.

"Spread your legs for me." His voice lowered, turning deep. "I need to taste every part of you."

Oh gosh, she must be in heaven. That she might be stuck with the living pushed through her heated thoughts and she ruthlessly shoved it away. She would enjoy this for all it was worth.

"Jess?"

She loved that he shortened her name when he totally focused on her. She spread her legs for him. The fact was, she loved too much about him, his caring, his smile, his sense of humor, even his arrogance.

Duncan repositioned his hands to hold her beneath her thighs, then he brought her to his face and his tongue shot out and flicked her clit.

She jerked as pure excitement spasmed across her groin. She loved his tongue. She must remember to add that to the list of what she loved about him.

That tongue began to explore her folds, licking between every one until it lapped up the juices seeping from her passage. She held on to his hair, loving her own weightlessness as he ate her, better than she'd imagined.

"Your taste is intoxicating." He spoke against her entrance, vibrations from his voice hitting sensitive spots all over her folds.

Then his hands grasped her harder and his tongue burrowed into her a bit at a time, moving in circles then pulling straight out and repeating it.

Her heartbeat kicked into overdrive, and though her hips moved against his hands, he kept her exactly where he wanted. A sudden swipe of his tongue, flat against her opening and up over her clit caught her by surprise. Her sheath clenched. "Oh yes."

Duncan repeated the action, then pushed his tongue inside her before lapping it up over her clit.

Her breaths were short as zings of pleasure pinged through her every time he thrust and lapped. He groaned with his tongue inside her, pulling her against his face as if he couldn't get enough.

Her body tightened, preparing. Duncan thrust and lapped again, then circled her clit, pushing it to and fro, its strength surprising her and flinging her closer to her orgasm.

Then he nibbled at her hard nub, his teeth scraping it lightly. Ecstasy crackled through her, splintering her into a thousand pieces of pure light. She floated in her euphoria, unaware of anything but the pleasure of satisfaction.

Then Duncan pulled her down and she opened her eyes. He wrapped her legs around him and held her against him. His own heart raced in his chest, matching hers, reassuring her they were still on the same plane.

His rigid cock against her stomach was proof enough that not only did he want her, but their lovemaking was far from over. He pulled her arms from around his neck. "Lie back."

She did as he asked, her legs still wrapped around his waist as if she lay on a table. There were definitely advantages to making love while phased. They needed no bed or chair or even any muscle strength to make love. The positions they could get into were infinite.

He stared at her body. His fingertips tracing a trail of touch all over her skin, her ribs, her neck, her shoulders, her waist, her belly button. She watched his hands as they made their light trek across her body, almost as if he were memorizing every inch of her.

She glanced up at his face to find his brow furrowed. Something was wrong, but even if she asked, her gut told her he wouldn't tell her. Then his fingers lightly brushed her nipples and she brought her gaze back to his touch. He held both breasts in his massive hands.

"A perfect handful." He grinned at her, though the look didn't quite reach his eyes. Something was going on in that brain of his and she resented it. She wanted all his attention.

She reached up and trailed a finger down the length of his cock. His fingers stilled on her hardened nubs even as he sucked in his breath.

"Ye are playing with fire, lass."

It was her turn to grin. "I like fire. It's bright, happy, lively, and all consuming."

His gaze flew to hers at her last word and the fear and confusion in his eyes startled her. She lay her hand over his heart. "Duncan, is everything all right?"

He left her breasts and grasped her hand against him with one hand while the other spread over her heart. "Aye. Everything is fine."

His look was far too serious for sexual play and she promised herself to enjoy him and not think about what it all meant beyond pleasure. She used her free hand to touch the top of his cock. The spot of pre-cum she swirled around the head reassured her he would want to continue.

His hand left her chest and grabbed her wrist. "I want to savor ye."

"And I want you deep inside me right now."

His eyes turned a dark blue at her words and his chest expanded with a deep breath. "Then we want the same things." His voice came out low, almost guttural and her whole body tingled, recognizing their mutual need.

Duncan let go of her hands and pushed her away, but just far enough to lower his cock between her legs. He pulled her back a few inches and rubbed his tip against her clit.

Spikes of need skittered inside her passage. The man had her wound tighter than a hauling winch and she was ready to snap. She hit his ass with her heel and tried to pull herself onto him.

He stopped her just as his cock slid down to her opening. "Shhh, slowly."

He would kill her with wanting, if she weren't already dead.

Maybe a little encouragement would help. She moved her hands up to her breasts and massaged them, not daring to touch her own nipples for fear she'd come again before he even entered her.

His groan was her only warning before he pulled her toward him, slowly moving deeper and deeper inside her, spreading her wide with the thickness of his erection. Every nerve ending in her entire body tingled, waiting.

She glanced up at Duncan and found his eyes closed, his jaw tense as he held her against him. If either of them moved she would come. She was so close. She let her gaze wander over his hard chest and stomach muscles. How did she get so lucky?

How did she fall so fast?

She bit down on her bottom lip to keep from crying out as the enormity of her situation hit her. She was in love with a man who didn't fall in love. And she was dead on the verge of being stuck with the living for eternity.

The tears welled as her sensitive body primed for the greatest joy. Then Duncan moved. His hands, gripping her hips, pushed her away and pulled her back in. It was the sweetest torture, as all the sparks ignited at once and he thrust again, this time faster and then faster, setting off her orgasm. She cried out.

She was engulfed in hot fire as he pumped into her, sending another wave of heat rolling through her, threatening to burn her from the inside out.

Then Duncan shouted and his come filled her, causing a chain reaction that burst inside her, turning her pleasure into a vortex of flame.

Duncan's thrusts became more uneven, and she felt as if she continued to be showered in the fragmented lights of sparklers, tiny pricks of pleasure still going off until Duncan slowed to a stop.

He gathered her up into his arms and kissed her. "Jess, ye amaze me."

She wrapped her arms around his neck and buried her face on his shoulder. The tears flowed. Too many emotions finding release once her body had been satisfied.

"Jess?" Duncan's concerned voice forced her to look at him.

"Ach, lass, I didn't hurt ye, did I?"

She shook her head and tried to smile. "That was just so beyond anything I've ever experienced."

A look of pure male satisfaction crossed his face, but she couldn't begrudge him that.

He brushed her hair away from her eyes. "It was for me too."

She couldn't help the doubt that crept into her voice. "Really?"

He nodded, his serious face revealing the confusion in his eyes.

She placed a hand on his cheek. "It's okay. I guess we are just a good fit." She wiggled her brows, trying desperately to lighten the mood.

He nodded absently before hugging her close again.

She had no problem with that. Being held to his hard body, still connected to him, was the perfect place for her. If only—

A scream rent the air.

Jessica leaned back. "That was Holly!"

Duncan pulled her off him, but despite her concern, irritation at having her own moment destroyed caught her off guard. How selfish was she?

Duncan phased his clothes on and sped away toward the scream.

She tried to phase hers on.

Shit. Her right sleeve appeared on her left arm, her panties on her right arm and her bra caught around her legs. Okay, maybe not the best time to try something new. She quickly disrobed and pulled on her clothes. She'd just finished buttoning the last button on her blouse as she drifted toward the edge of the hill when Duncan floated up, Holly holding his hand and looking very pale.

They stopped in front of her. She moved toward Holly to give her a hug, but caught Duncan shaking his head. Stifling her need to comfort, she made herself stay where she was. "Are you okay?"

Holly nodded, still holding Duncan's hand. She could let go anytime now. "What happened?"

Holly looked at Duncan.

"She ran into some ghosts."

Jessica swallowed hard. "Were they scary ghosts?"

Holly finally let go of Duncan's hand and crossed her arms. "I'll say. They were bloody and old. Seriously, they could have come from a horror movie."

"What she saw was the English soldiers who were killed by Robert the Bruce and his men at a battle that took place here in 1307."

"They're still here?"

He nodded as Holly rolled her eyes. "Oh, they are definitely still here."

Jessica looked at Duncan. "But how can Holly see them?"

He floated closer to her. "Because she's phased. If she decided to take a hike up this hill tomorrow morning, she wouldn't even know they are here."

"Oh, yes I would, and there is no way I'm ever coming back here."

That could be a good thing. Jessica glanced at Duncan and they shared an understanding. If Holly wouldn't come back to the place where Cameron proposed to her because of the ghosts, the next spirits might actually be able to help her. It loosened a worry Jessica had deep in her heart.

Duncan took her hand. "Holly, we'll be right back. You stay right here while we discuss the next stop."

Holly's brows furrowed but she nodded.

Duncan pulled Jessica over to the small monolith that marked the top of the hill. "We are going to bring her to her second to last Christmas Eve with Cameron, but—"

"Why not her last Christmas Eve? I would think that would hold stronger happiness for her since it was the last they shared together."

"I think so too." Duncan pulled at the neckline on his t-shirt. "But Cameron insisted on the Christmas before. Of course, he wouldn't tell me why." Duncan's frustration was clear in his face.

"Did he tell you why he was testing me?"

"No." He hesitated. "He did admit this case is special and reassured me he had permission to take it, but he was different." Duncan looked away for a moment then returned his gaze to her. "It was as if he were a completely different person. He's always calm, but when I confronted him, he turned aggressive."

"Maybe that's because his wife is involved. With the love they had for each other, I could see him being very protective."

"That could be, but I think it's more. Something else is happening here and I wonder if even he has any control over it."

Jessica shuddered. "That's concerning."

"It is. But I still need to find out what we need to do to bring you back to the afterlife before it's too late."

"I don't want to be stuck here." She couldn't keep her voice from shaking.

He pulled her into his embrace. "I know. And I won't let you. I will make Cameron tell me. And if he refuses, I'll go over his head. I won't let you be trapped here, but you have to do your part too."

"Disconnect from Holly."

"You can do it. You just need to have faith that what you have done so far for her and your counsel through the rest will set her up for her next visits. Remember, you dinna have to solve all her problems."

She nodded unenthusiastically.

"Lass, look at me."

She raised her gaze to his. There was so much concern in his eyes, she could really believe he cared for her. Maybe he did, like a friend. That did lighten her heart a bit.

"Remember the night of Holly's fire? You did what you could and it set her and her mother on a positive path for their lives. This is what you must do here. Set her on the path and let others have a chance to help her too."

"Wow, I never thought about it that way. That's how it worked with Mrs. Connors as well, but I hadn't known that." She studied him, a new appreciation for his abilities growing. "I guess there's a reason you train Spirit Guides."

He raised his brows. "Did you ever doubt there was?"

She smiled. How could she not with him sporting such a shit-eating grin. "Frankly, yes, but I admit to being wrong."

He pulled away and stared at her in shock.

She frowned. "Don't you say a word. Not one word, Duncan Montgomerie."

He burst into laughter, the sound rippling through her and soothing her heart.

He pulled her to him. "Then you'll just have to kiss me to keep me quiet."

She wrapped her arms around his neck and gladly complied. As his tongue breached her lips, she met it with her own and melted into him, her stomach flipping over with desire.

When he finally broke the kiss, she sighed. No wonder the man had slept his way through so many beds in the last two hundred years. What woman could resist him?

"If you keep giving me that look, lass, I'll be making love to ye right here in front of Holly."

She dropped her arms and looked over her shoulder to see Holly wasn't even facing them. She turned back to him only to catch his wide smile and silent chuckle. "Not funny."

He shrugged. "It wasn't supposed to be. I meant it."

Mr. Obsession was becoming far too sure of himself. "I don't think we should." She let her gaze roam from his blue eyes down to his sock-covered feet. She returned her gaze to his, a little disappointed his smile had disappeared. "As much as I'd like to, we've made Holly wait far too long. We are in her time right now and I'm sure she is anxious to see another moment in her past."

Duncan's face remained serious. Was he still with her?

"Aye, you're right. We need to complete this assignment as soon as we can. I'm going to escort you both to the next Christmas Eve, but you are to keep her outside her home until I return."

She tensed. "You're going to talk to Cameron again?"

"This time, I promise I won't leave until I get answers as long as you promise no' to go inside Holly's house no matter how much she begs." He grasped her shoulders. "Can you do that? Can you deny her to save your soul?"

She definitely wanted to. She just wasn't sure if and when the time came, she could. "I promise I will do everything in my power to resist giving in to her."

"That's no' good enough." Duncan's eyes intensified, their blue becoming brighter. "You must promise you will no' give in to her. This may very well be what Cameron is testing you on."

"Do you think so?"

He nodded.

She hadn't thought Cameron would feel the need to test her ability to remain professional. She had been so focused on the big picture and doing whatever was necessary to achieve it, that she missed the fact her new supervisor may very well be testing protocol points or task management. She was such an idiot. "I promise I will deny Holly entrance to her home until you come back."

Duncan's hands loosened and he patted her shoulder. "Good. Now let's get Holly."

Chapter Nine

Duncan raced back to Cameron's office. The second Jessica had asked him to make love to her, he understood why. Her face had revealed no' only her fear but a hopelessness that triggered a long-forgotten concern of his own. He'd known that feeling, but he couldn't remember why. It had been so long. It frustrated him that there were now parts of his life he couldn't recall. Some were no' important, but that feeling was.

He sped toward Cameron's office. Last time he'd stormed in, concern for Jessica and distrust of Cameron's motives were at the forefront of his mind. That hadn't worked.

Now he was far beyond concerned. He was as afraid as she was. He could lose her forever. The pain in his chest shook his soul.

He halted, floating in darkness between planes as a memory brushed by. He'd felt like this before when he was alive.

He embraced the fear and deep-seated terror that he couldn't do anything about it, hoping to bring the memory to full fruition. But it drifted by, leaving a gut-wrenching pain that took his breath away. He leaned forward, hands on his knees as he tried to breathe. No air filled his lungs and blackness took his peripheral vision. Whispers seeped into his head of souls disappearing. The darkness grew, his feet melding with time so they no longer appeared.

Breathe. He had to breathe. He had to save Jessica. Blast it!

"Jessica!"

The darkness disappeared, the whispers vanished and a dull pain took residence in the back of his head as air slammed into his lungs. He coughed, causing the pain to pulse.

He had no doubt that to solidify would mean a pain so great he would pass out. He didn't dare allow that. He had to save Jessica and fast. His heart raced as new knowledge permeated his consciousness. He didn't have much time.

He was ceasing to exist.

That's what Cameron didn't want to tell him.

He started for his friend's office. If this was the end to his soul, he had to make sure Jessica was safe first. The ache in his chest grew. He wanted to be with her. How could he have found someone so perfect for him only to cease to exist? He fisted his hands even as he accepted the irony.

When he arrived at Cameron's office, an anguished resignation had fallen over him and he calmly walked in when bid to enter.

"Duncan." Cameron's surprise was followed by lowered brows.

He strode forward, his hands out as if he could pacify his supervisor and friend. "I need your help."

Cameron looked down at his paperwork. "I thought I told you to do whatever it takes to finish Holly's visits."

Duncan sat in the chair across from the cluttered desk. He'd never even considered what Cameron's job must be like. How many Spirit Guides did he command? A hundred? A thousand? Yet, they had been friends since he'd arrived. "Cameron, Holly is learning. It's working."

The man lifted his face from the paperwork and met Duncan's gaze and for a tenth of a second, Duncan witnessed a soul-deep torment in Cameron's eyes before it was hidden and a slight smile curved his lips. "She is? That's my Holly."

Duncan smiled encouragingly. If Jessica was his primary focus,

Holly was Cameron's. "Aye, we are on the last event and I think she's even taught Jessica and me a thing or two."

Cameron leaned back. "Really?"

Duncan nodded. "One of the reasons Holly has done so well is her connection to Jessica. You knew she would remember Jessica and have an openness to her, didn't you?"

"Yes, I did."

"Did you know Jessica would have an equally strong connection to Holly?"

Cameron nodded.

Duncan used all his willpower no' to let his voice rise in anger. "Did you know Jessica would transform into a ghost because of it?"

The man's eyes widened. "No. How?"

"She was good as a social worker while she was alive because she personally cared about every client she had. These visits you arranged for Holly that connect to Jessica have undermined a lot of what she was proud of."

"But they've shown her what she thought were failures were actually successes."

Duncan's mind raced. So this was as much about Jessica as Holly. "Aye, but now she wonders how many of her successes were failures. And now she is stuck on the plane with the living, but she isn't a ghost yet. Tell me there's a chance we can bring her back."

Cameron's concern was obvious. "This wasn't supposed to happen. We have to get her back."

Hope flickered like an almost-lit candle before him. "So we can bring her back."

"Yes. But the only way to do that is if she has a connection with this plane that is stronger than her connection with Holly."

"Like what?"

Cameron leaned forward. "Like her cottage or her position, or you."

"Me? What do you mean me?"

Cameron's gaze was intense. "Does she think of you like a case?"

From what he could discern, she hadn't even tried to counsel him. Maybe she recognized a lost cause. The thought was disturbing. "No, she accepts me for the way I am." Now wasn't that a positive spin on a lousy truth.

"What about sexually? That's your specialty. Have you connected with her strong enough on a sexual level?"

Duncan tensed. "That's no' for you to inquire about."

Cameron stood, slamming his hands down on the desk. "If you haven't established that connection, then you had better have established an emotional one or the woman is lost to us. And she is a damn good Spirit Guide."

Duncan's anger had him rising as well. "She's more than her job. She's a warmhearted, caring, beautiful soul and deserves all the help we can give her because she's worth saving simply because of who she is."

Cameron smiled. "So you love her."

It was as if Cameron had kicked him in the chest. His heart hurt and the ache in the back of his head throbbed anew. "How would I know? I've never loved anyone."

Disappointment shone in Cameron's gaze. "So you still don't remember how you died, even after over two hundred years."

"What? I thought we aren't supposed to remember that."

"You're wrong." Cameron shook his head. "Your supervisors in the past have been so happy with your performance, they haven't counseled you as they should have. I'm not that selfish."

"What do you mean counseled? I dinna need counseling. I'm the one to do that for the living and the mentees."

"That's where you're wrong. My job is to counsel the Spirit Guide Mentors to help you move on."

Every muscle in Duncan's body tensed. "What do you mean move on? Do you mean these episodes I'm having where I start to disintegrate? If that's what you're talking about, I'm afraid you are a bit too late. It's already happening." He gave a scornful laugh. "Guess I didn't need counseling after all."

Cameron phased through the desk and grabbed him by the shoulders. "Is it getting worse?" The concern in his eyes soothed Duncan's taut nerves.

He looked away. "Aye. On my way here I almost lost it." He returned his gaze to Cameron. "But I knew I had to save Jessica before I let it take me."

Relief flickered in Cameron's concerned eyes. "That's not the moving on I was hoping for. This means you must save Jessica with Holly's last visit. Do whatever it takes, because no one else here can save her. If she means anything to you—"

He shook off Cameron's hands. "She means more to me than she does to you."

"Good. Tell her. Tell her you love her and hopefully she feels something too."

"Hopefully?" Duncan didn't like that. "And I willna lie to her. I dinna know what it feels like to love and she knows that."

Cameron drifted back through his desk and solidified again. "You do."

Duncan blinked. "I do what?"

"You do know what love feels like. You died for love."

He desperately tried to think back, but no memory of his death came to him. It had been far too long. "Tell me."

Cameron shook his head. "I can't." Though he didn't look at him, his tone was touched with anguish. He really couldn't. Blast, the rules in the afterlife were far more complicated than the rules of the living during his life.

If he could just picture what he was doing, but all that came to him was his castle. He rose, drifting into the desk. "Can you at least tell me where I died?"

"I don't—" Cameron's gaze returned to his. "Actually." He seemed to ponder something. Maybe the man had the rule book in his head and was looking for a loophole. He certainly hoped so.

Cameron smiled. "Yes, you were at a burn near your castle."

Hope, that tiny candle flame, grew stronger. Duncan nodded his appreciation and floated home to Rossan Castle.

~~*~~

Jessica brought Holly down to the town square in quaint Deervale. There was the lightest snow falling, not even accumulating where the cars drove and the people walked, but it looked pretty as it reflected the Christmas lights along the streets surrounding them in the dimmer light of an overcast day.

Holly grinned. "Look. There's Mrs. Branson." She pointed to an elderly lady making her way along a sidewalk. "Her scooter looks brand new. We must be just a couple years back." Holly turned to face Jessica. "Right?"

"Yes, I believe this was your first Christmas as a married couple."

Holly's gaze drifted away as a slight smile curved her lips.

Had she ever had that look on her own face? Jessica shook her head. That was doubtful. She spent her life loving her work, not loving a person. She had to admit what she'd felt for Jacob wasn't what she saw on Holly's face. Now if she considered Duncan Montgomerie…

She tensed. She couldn't be thinking about him like that, even if her feelings for him were already far stronger than any she had in her lifetime. He would finish this assignment with her, hopefully figure out how she could get back to the afterlife, and then move on to his next mentee.

She rubbed at her chest at the pain it gave her to think of him with a new woman Spirit Guide. He might make an effort to be friends with her while he worked with another newbie, but even now she was sure she couldn't handle it. Shit. When had she fallen for him?

"Jessica?"

"Yes."

"I called you three times." Holly appeared concerned. "Where were you?"

With Duncan Montgomerie. "Sorry, I was thinking about a problem I have."

Holly winked. "That problem wouldn't happen to be a Scottish spirit with a heavy accent, would it?"

"Holly." She kept her tone stern, like she would use with a misbehaving child.

Holly shrugged. "It's pretty obvious you two have something going on. The way you look at him and the way he devours you when you're not looking."

Jessica flushed. "I'm thinking you're seeing more than there is. We both know he's a Romeo."

Holly shook her head. "I'm not so sure. He really seems into you."

At Holly's phrase her memory reproduced the feelings of what it felt like to have Duncan thrusting *into* her and her pulse sped. "Well, we aren't here to discuss Duncan. He's been around for over two hundred years and is still single, so I'm guessing that isn't going to change anytime soon. So let's focus on why you caught my attention."

"Oh right. I was just pointing out Mrs. Bell." Holly turned back to look at the busy square. "There." She pointed at a woman, maybe in her forties, with two strapping young men following her, their hands filled with bags. "She's one of my neighbors and makes the best food. After Cameron died, you'd think she wanted me to double in size with all the things she cooked for me." Holly chuckled. "I had to freeze most of it."

"You look as trim as ever. How did you get her to stop feeding you?"

"I didn't completely. She still brings over food on holidays. But, well, I kind of told her about Mr. Wrenford who is this old bachelor, and I might have intimated that he ate out a lot and maybe I assumed he would love a home-cooked meal."

Jessica grinned. "You lied."

Holly tried to frown, but finally gave Jessica a sheepish look. "I stretched the truth a wee bit."

"A wee bit?"

"Aye, that's what yer supposed to say in Scotland."

Jessica chuckled at Holly's attempt at a Scottish accent. "Maybe you should stick to the American version."

"Probably. Oh look. That's Brody and his girlfriend." Holly's eyes gleamed with excitement. "This was the last year we had everyone over for Christmas Eve. Come on, we have to go to the house."

Jessica grasped Holly's arm. "Not yet. We have to wait for Duncan."

"Can we at least walk down the street toward the house?"

That seemed acceptable. They weren't going into the house. "Sure, we can do that."

The two of them drifted across the street, Holly pointing out people along the way.

"You've come to know quite a few people in the few years you've been here."

"I guess I have. But it's a small town, so it wasn't hard and everyone was so nice." Holly paused. "Or rather most people were nice."

Jessica followed Holly's gaze to see a young woman heading toward them. She had bright-red hair that flowed to her shoulders, a long but beautiful face and she was thin enough to be a model. "Who's that?"

"That's Sofia Dunlap. No matter how hard I try, I just don't like her."

"Any particular reason why? Is she rude? Snobby?"

"No." Sofia walked by them, her stride confident and brisk. "She's just too self-involved. She can't see past that pretty nose of hers. She never voluntarily helps anyone and can't think beyond her own needs." Holly sighed. "Unfortunately, she's set her sights on Ethan."

"Who's Ethan?"

"One of Cam's two best friends." She pointed ahead of them. "That's Brody, his other best friend. He's just like Cam, always up for another venture. The lady on his arm is Sarah. He's still seeing her, the last I heard."

Jessica halted and grasped Holly. "What do you mean, you've heard? Don't they talk to you anymore?"

Holly wouldn't look her in the eye. "Of course they do, I've just been busy running the shop by myself."

"Uh-huh. It's more than that. Tell me."

Holly faced her. "It's hard to be around them. They remind me so much of Cam, especially Brody. They invite me to gatherings and such, but…it's just hard."

Jessica's heart swelled a bit at the obvious anguish on Holly's face. Though she wanted to give her a hug, Duncan's words resounded in her head. *You just need to have faith that what you have done so far for her and your counsel through the rest will set her up for her next visits. Remember, you dinna have to solve all her problems.* She settled for a hand on Holly's shoulder. "I understand."

"You do?" Hope filled Holly's pretty brown eyes.

Jessica nodded. "Yes, I do. It hasn't been long enough and your loss is still raw. Just don't cut these two friends off completely so that when you are able to be around them, you can benefit from their support."

Holly nodded. "I promise to stay in touch with them."

"Good. I imagine if they were as good of friends as you say, they are hurting a lot too. I bet they want to be around you because it helps them feel closer to Cameron."

Holly's eyes widened. "I never thought about it from their point of view, but that does make a lot of sense. Thank you."

Jessica smiled. "For what?"

"For helping me see the situation from someone else's point of view. I was being a bit like Sofia Dunlap, all wrapped up in myself."

"I don't think the comparison is entirely fair."

A loud laugh behind them had them both turning. Holly groaned. "Speak of the devil."

"Is that Ethan?"

Holly nodded. "Yes. Luckily he brought Cameron's cousin to our party. There is no relationship there, but it looks like he's making it appear that way in front of Sophia. Good for him."

Jessica studied the young man. He was incredibly good-looking, with curly hair and a face that resembled Michelangelo's David. It begged the question, was his body as similar to that famous statue?

Holly said this man was the complete opposite of Cameron. He was also very opposite in looks. Cameron had a hardness about his looks, though his face softened incredibly around Holly. Who Cameron's friends were might give her insight into how to handle her new boss. That was, if she still had one. If she remained among the living as a ghost, she wouldn't have a boss anymore, or a purpose.

She shivered, her gut tightening as fear raced through her chest. Where was Duncan? He should have returned to them by now. He could move through time easily, so why hadn't he rejoined them?

Unless Cameron was testing her.

But would he really test her at the cost of his wife's happiness? From the love she'd seen on his face that brief moment she'd stopped in to see Holly and found him there, he would never sacrifice Holly's happiness.

"Good." Holly nodded as Ethan and his "date" passed by. "He did that perfectly. Did you see her invite herself to our party?"

Jessica shook her head. "No, I missed that."

Holly looked at her quizzically. "Jessica, you're very distracted. Is something wrong?"

"I'm sorry. I just have a lot on my mind." She started to float down the sidewalk, forcing Holly to come along. "So was this the first Christmas for your shop?"

"No, this was our second year. The first year we barely had enough ornaments and decorations to fill a third of the shop. It took longer than we expected to make arrangements with artists and craftsmen." Holly's smile was full of pride. "We only sell one-of-a-kind Christmas items. That's why all of our items are handmade. We even have contracts with our suppliers that they will not make another item exactly the same. Some may be similar, but not exact."

"Wow, I didn't realize that. You have a very special shop."

She grinned. "We do. It's one of a kind."

Jessica rolled her eyes at Holly's smirk.

She burst out laughing. "I never get tired of saying that."

They drifted to a stop in front of the One of a Kind Christmas Shop. Holly crossed her arms. "It took a lot of work, late nights, and negotiations to make this successful. But it finally happened."

"It's Cameron's legacy to you."

Holly nodded silently, her eyes tearing. "It is. I will never sell it. As long as it's keeping a roof over my head, I will keep it open, in memory of him."

Jessica stifled her urge to put her arms around Holly's shoulders. She needed to keep her distance.

"Can we go in? It's not as full as I made it this year. I just couldn't stop buying more items."

The shop was attached to the house, but it wasn't the house, so Jessica nodded. Helping Holly look at the shop as Cameron's legacy would only help her.

They floated through the large glass picture window. Inside were a number of last-minute shoppers.

"Oh look, Brody brought Sarah here. I think that was their first Christmas as a couple." Holly drifted toward Cam's best friend.

Jessica grinned. For a woman who didn't want to be around Cameron's buddies, she unconsciously gravitated toward them. Maybe it was time for her to rejoin them.

Brody was built like Cameron, muscular and athletic, but his features were quite different. His hair was a very light brown, almost blond color. He had high cheek bones and his mouth seemed to be perpetually smiling. He showed Sarah an ornament, turning on the little lights that flickered inside it, causing him to laugh.

Jessica left Holly to enjoy this special time watching her friends explore her own shop. As she floated toward the front, she slowed to watch a slightly younger Holly wrap an ornament for a very pregnant woman. Holly glowed with warmth and happiness. The younger Holly was so different from the Holly she'd first glimpsed when she and Duncan looked in on her in this shop.

She looked back at Holly now, smiling as she watched Ethan show Cameron's cousin a reindeer that moved.

They had really made a difference for Cameron's wife and Jessica was more than a little proud of that. The next spirits had a lot to work with. Now if Duncan would only come, they could finish the final visit.

She floated outside as if being there would make him come

sooner. It was growing dark, a clear sign Duncan had been gone far too long. Was Cameron being stubborn? Had Duncan had another of his zombie-like happenings that kept him from traveling to the right time?

She drifted farther down the sidewalk toward the square. She missed him. That thought stopped her forward motion. She must be losing her mind. It was one thing to fall for the man, but to miss him after what couldn't be more than an hour was just plain pathetic.

Somehow, she didn't think Holly would think her pathetic.

Resolutely, she turned back. That was because Holly was a sweetheart who smiled at everyone, even when she didn't feel like smiling. Maybe after this last visit, she could smile a little easier.

As Jessica approached the shop, Holly floated out. "There you are. We have to go in the house now. Everyone's there except me."

She shook her head. "No we have to wait for Duncan. Remember what happened last time we didn't wait?"

"You mean you got in trouble for taking me on an unscheduled stop."

Jessica bit her tongue from explaining any further. "Yes."

"But this is my last visit. I don't want to miss it. It's not like I'll ever have this opportunity again."

"But Holly, we can simply bring you back an hour and you can be inside the house from the beginning." She smiled to soften her refusal.

"Then can we go back an hour now? I wouldn't mind checking in on some friends since I can basically be in two places at once now."

Could she? As a living person who was phased, could she "relive" the last hour? One way to find out. "Why not? Take my hand."

Jessica started back in time only to feel Holly's hand slip from hers. No! Her heartbeat went into double time as she raced forward again.

"…sica! Oh good, you're still here. You scared me disappearing like that."

"Are you okay?"

"Of course, I'm fine. So are we going?"

She shook her head. "It won't work. I just tried. That's why I disappeared, but you couldn't come with me."

Holly's eyes widened. "That means I'm missing my last chance to see Cameron alive." She looked next door to her home.

Shit. Where was Duncan? She needed him here in more ways than one.

Holly didn't try to argue with her for a change. Instead, she moved toward the front window and stared inside.

Jessica's stomach ached for her. If this was the event Holly was supposed to see and she didn't see it, what would Cameron think then? Where was Duncan? He said not to go in and then he doesn't arrive in Holly's timeline to go in with them?

He didn't want her to give in to Holly because she'd grown close to her. That was true, but now she had full faith in Holly's ability to overcome her sorrow with further visits from other spirits. She wouldn't be giving in to Holly. She'd be doing her job.

Floating to where Holly stood, her gaze glued to the happenings inside, she grasped her hand. "Ready to go inside?"

"Really? What about Duncan?"

"I don't know what happened to him, but I do know Cameron would be really mad at me if you didn't get to experience this final visit. So shall we?"

Holy's smile was wide as she nodded.

"You bet."

Chapter Ten

Duncan didn't bother entering his home. Instead he phased into his kilt and linen shirt. For the first time since being assigned Holly's case, he felt like he could breathe without the tight-feeling material about his chest, arms and neck. Modern clothes were far too restrictive.

Floating across the fields near his castle, he headed for the largest burn on his property. There was a sturdy bridge across it on the south side, but even before he reached it, he changed his direction and floated farther south. Along the water's edge on the castle's side, though a dirt road hugged the other side.

He hovered near a spot where the embankment had no trees or bushes on either side and felt the back of his head. The hidden pain had vanished. Drifting to the ground, he solidified.

It had been raining that day. No' exactly an uncommon occurrence, but something about the rain had been uncommon. Too much? Too little?

Too much. Too many days of rain. Months of rain. He looked at the calmly weaving water's surface. It hadn't looked like this. Images of rushing water flashed across his mind. Aye, the burn had been a torrent. Worse than ever seen before.

He glanced back at the bridge. No, the bridge had stayed. So why was the burn so important? It hadn't overflowed this far inland.

He looked again at the embankment across from him. He'd been here, stood here.

His heartbeat increased. The opposite side had given way, part of the road sheering off and something terrible had happened. A carriage had tilted into the water, but even as he stood there he was sure he hadn't been in it. Why was the carriage important?

There were people in the carriage, coming to see him, but as hard as he concentrated he couldn't see their faces. He could hear screaming. He had to help.

His chest filled with terror, but as he stood looking at the placid surface, he couldn't bring the memory up. Why had he been so afraid? What had he done?

He whipped around. Had he been attacked? Even at that thought, he shook his head. He looked back at the opposite river bank. He'd been here, standing here. The screaming started again, urging him to action, to do something? What did he do? Why?

He turned away from the bank, walking away. He *had* to remember. Cameron had said he'd loved once, but he couldn't remember ever loving a woman. He halted. That was why he recognized the hopelessness in Jessica's eyes.

He had felt that. He had given up finding a woman to love. Once he'd stopped looking, he'd been able to enjoy life, taking all it had to offer, minus a companion to grow old with. He'd thrown himself into every experience, hunting, fishing, playing golf, dancing, drinking, sex. But he never stayed long enough to fall in love, convinced he wanted the unobtainable. He'd been right. He had wanted what Cameron and Holly had.

He never found it. Of that, he was absolutely sure.

He strode back toward the burn. The upturned carriage was the key. Cameron said he'd loved. As he approached it again, the screaming filled his head. It was a woman. She was beautiful despite her wet hair and soaked gown. He focused on her. He'd known her intimately, but he had no' loved her. Just another woman among many he had lain with. He stepped to the edge again and the need to take action struck him hard. He was desperate, but why? For what?

He fisted his hands as he dropped to his knees, frustration and anger surging through him. Why couldn't he remember?

White-hot pain filled his head. "Nay!" He grabbed it and phased, the pain immediately lessening. He took his hands away from his head and stared. They were wavy again. If he went to Jessica like this, she wouldn't be able to see him. He had to hold on just a little longer. Blackness started to enshroud him, the burn slowly disappearing.

He couldn't let it go. It was an important part of remembering, in order to save Jessica. Despite the agony that waited for him in a puddle at the back of his skull, he needed to become solid to thwart the darkness. A tiny part of the flowing burn still within his vision assured him he remained in the afterlife plane.

He solidified.

Razor sharp shards splintered through his head and he moaned, but he refused to phase. He bent over, burying his hands in the grass, digging his fingers into the dirt to withstand the agony. He held on, determined to stay solid and in the afterlife. He refused to be taken away yet. His tensed biceps grew tired as he grasped hard to his land, refusing the painless darkness. He forced his muscles to hold on… like he had once before. Right here.

The muscle memory triggered another. It hadn't happened on the bank. He'd been swimming in the burn, through the raging water. It was imperative he keep his head up. He had to stay alive. Is that what Cameron meant, that he loved himself?

He brushed the idea aside. It didn't feel right. It was something else. He'd taken action to conquer the terror he'd felt. He hadn't been afraid of the waters. He'd been motivated by something else, something…love.

Peace soothed the pain radiating through him, allowing him to release the earth and sit back on his haunches. He *had* loved. He still didn't know who, but the memory of that feeling grew in his heart. Relief, hope, wonder swelled inside him. If he had loved before, he could again.

Duncan jumped up, his body rejuvenated. He could save Jessica if she'd been able to disconnect from Holly. The blasted "episodes" messed with his time abilities. He just hoped that too much time hadn't passed among the living. He'd try to get as close to when he left the women in the town square as he could get.

He just needed to reach her before he was taken by the darkness. Even as he flew through space and time, his gut twisted. He didn't want to be taken. He had something worth existing for now. Something special he'd never had while alive and he wanted to experience it to the fullest.

As he sped over Scotland toward Deervale, he tried to put together the instances that had triggered all his pain and one thing stood out. Each time he'd been emotionally charged. When he won the bet against Cameron for the first time, he'd been elated. On the castle roof he'd been ready to come inside Jessica. Anger, frustration and a combination of the two had set off the other episodes.

Did that mean he couldn't feel the love forming in his heart without the pain and darkness? Doubt clouded his view for a moment before he recognized the square where he'd left the women.

Only Christmas lights blinked in the silent night. No one was there. Blast.

Jessica and Holly floated next to the Christmas tree watching the antics of Holly's friends. It was clear the three men were very close and the women got along well as women do at parties, but they obviously weren't friends outside of these gatherings. Holly said

Brody was still seeing Sarah, so this must have been early in their relationship.

Cameron's cousin, Brooke, kept glancing at Ethan. "Holly, I think Cameron's cousin is more interested in Ethan than he realizes."

Holly turned her gaze from staring at Cameron to watch Brooke. "Oh wow, you're right. I never noticed."

Jessica winked. "Probably because you were too googly eyed over Cameron."

She blushed, but didn't deny it. How could she, even at the gathering her gaze drifted to him regularly. "I hope Ethan catches on. He needs a woman in his life. He dates, but none of them seem to stick."

The men called the women over to take seats and the gift exchange began.

Holly floated to where her former self sat, cuddled up to Cameron in their love seat. Sarah sat in one of the chairs while Brody perched on the arm. Ethan stood next to the chair where Brooke sat.

Jessica drifted back toward the kitchen, her worry about Duncan growing. He should have arrived by now. While she had the ability to still move through time and space among the living, so she could return Holly, she couldn't then return to the afterlife. Unless…

Maybe since she felt Holly was well on her way, her connection had diminished. She glanced at Holly, who remained riveted to the party. No time like the present to try. Focusing her mind on her little cottage she flew up through the roof of the house toward her own little home. The darkness of time swept by and then she landed.

In Holly's house exactly when she'd left.

Fear grew deep in her belly and she pushed her glasses up as she turned away from the happy scene in the living room. Why couldn't she leave? She had faith the next spirits could help Holly further.

She planned to ask Cameron if she could serve as Holly's Spirit of Christmas Present, but if not, she would ask to be part of his decision on who to send. That's how she'd done it when she was alive. As the social worker passing along the case, she always had a say in who would best work it. Well, not always, but certainly most of the time. It was in the best interest of the client.

"Jessica, you've got to watch this." Holly's voice was filled with undisguised anticipation.

She turned back toward her and drifted into the living room again. "What am I watching?"

"What Brody got us for Christmas."

Jessica smiled at Holly's excitement and watched as Cameron opened a box with an envelope in it. He glanced up at his friend. "A card? You shouldn't have."

Brody laughed. "Open it, smart arse."

Cameron proceeded to, making a big production of it. When he opened the card, a certificate fell out. He picked it up and immediately lost his grin. "We can't accept this."

"What is it?" Ethan took a step closer.

The young Holly stared open-mouthed.

Cameron addressed Ethan. "It's a week stay at Dailloch Castle hotel."

Jessica inhaled hard. She had planned to stay there, but work had once again called her more strongly. If she remembered correctly, it had been a pregnant teenager thrown out of her parents' house with nowhere to go.

Ethan whistled then turned to Brody. "What did you do, sell your flat? Are you living in your car now?"

Brody laughed, obviously fully enjoying the awe he'd created. "Ach, no. My friend manages the place, so I got a really good deal."

Young Holly spoke up. "But Brody, that's still expensive. I hear their cheapest room is almost a thousand pounds a night. That's where all the American stars stay who don't want anyone to know they are there. It's got those huge walls around the property, which helps. Even if you got this for half off, it's still too much. We can't accept it."

Brody sobered. "You two never got to take your honeymoon because you put all your money into that fantastic shop next door. I want you to have a decent honeymoon."

Both Hollys teared up. Even Jessica found herself swallowing hard.

Cameron held out the certificate. "We really appreciate the thought, but it's too much. Do you think you can get your money back?"

Brody folded his arms. "I can't."

Young Holly gasped. "Why not?"

"Ach, you're making me spill it all, aren't you?" He threw up his arms. "Fine. It didn't cost me anything. Some rich American who scheduled two weeks canceled. Said he broke up with his girlfriend but had a new one and booked a week a month later. My friend told him he'd lose his deposit, but he didn't care. So there was one week already paid for and no one to use it. But you have to go over Hogmanay as that was the week that was paid for."

Cameron stood and gave his friend a heartfelt hug before young Holly followed.

Jessica barely noticed. The timing was too perfect. Jacob's father had died leaving him a huge inheritance and they were supposed to spend two weeks in Scotland, over New Year's. A month later he said he had a business trip. Was it just coincidence?

Her gut said no, and an angry burn started in the pit of her stomach, not at Jacob, but at Cameron. He just had to throw it in her face one more time that Jacob wasn't faithful. Well, she certainly hadn't been either. She'd been married to her job. If she'd spent any time with him, she would have figured it all out years ago.

Or did she drive Jacob to it by ignoring him? She shook her head. No, she wasn't taking the blame for that. He knew what he was getting into, and from Holly's first Christmas party, he saw other women while supposedly in love with her.

"Jessica, are you okay?"

She refocused her attention on Holly. "Yes, I'm fine."

"You don't look fine. You've faded more."

Her heart raced even before she focused on her hands. Holly was right. She *had* faded more.

"Jessica, what's happening?"

Tears threatened, but she had to remain calm. "It's okay. Don't worry. I just need to get you back to your own time. Are you ready to go?"

"What about Duncan?"

Jessica's heart twisted with despair. He must not have been able to find a way to help her and couldn't face her with his failure. She really would have liked to see him one more time.

She pulled her glasses off and hid her tears by pretending to clean the lenses on her blouse. At least they'd made love. At least, like Holly, she'd known what it was like to truly love someone even if he never loved her back. It wasn't his fault. He just wasn't programmed that way.

Settling her glasses on her nose, she took a deep breath and looked at Holly. "Are you ready?"

"Jessica!"

Duncan floated through the front window, his heart breaking as he took in everything in one glance. She'd given in to Holly and was already starting to fade. He couldn't let her be a ghost. To no' be able to hold her in his arms again would be torture. Is this what Cameron felt?

"Duncan, where have you been?" The anguish in her eyes destroyed any anger he had because she'd been swayed by Holly. It was simply who she was.

"Yes, where have you been?" Holly crossed her arms. "If it wasn't for Jessica, I would have missed my entire last visit."

He ignored Holly and grasped Jessica's hand. He could still feel it, but it wasn't completely solid. His heart tumbled with fear.

"I was worried about you." She looked back and forth at his eyes. "Did you have another…um, headache?"

Blast, the woman was fading into a ghost and she was worried about him? "Yes, and it affected my ability to come to you at the proper time. This was the closest I could get."

She looked over at Holly, who continued to scowl at him. "We were just going back to her place so she could resume solidity."

He nodded. She'd realized she was fading and wanted Holly to be safe. How could a woman with such a heart be trapped as a ghost? He wanted to rail at Cameron, but right now he had two women dependent on him.

"Holly, lass. Take my hand and we'll get you home to the right time."

Reluctantly, she grasped his free hand. Immediately, he flew them forward in time, not even trying for a different spot. Within seconds they were in Holly's house, in the same place. He loosened his hand from Holly and put it on her shoulder.

In seconds she was solid again.

"That was an amazing night." She glanced at the clock. "Oh wow, it's not even midnight yet."

Duncan stared at the clock. It was five minutes before midnight. A sinking feeling settled in his soul. If he couldn't reverse Jessica's fading before midnight, she would stay a ghost forever.

"So now what?" Holly looked around expectantly. "Do you two fly off and I go on with my lonely life?"

"No." Jessica tried to pull her hand from his to go to Holly, but he held firm.

"Yes." He pointed to Jessica. "As you can see, she needs help.

If I can't break her connection to you in the next five minutes she will be doomed to haunt you for eternity."

"Me?" Holly stepped back. "Why me?"

"Because she cares so much about you, she put your needs above her own."

Holly's face softened. "Jessica, you shouldn't have done that. I'm a strong woman. I will figure things out…eventually."

"But you were so sad." Jessica's voice sounded confused.

"Oh I was, and I still am, but I have a much better perspective on my life thanks to you. Please, you have done so much for me in my lifetime. I'm incredibly grateful. I would hate it if you were hurt because of me."

Duncan gave Holly an encouraging smile. He needed her to break the tie first.

Holly's eyes widened just slightly as understanding dawned. She moved to her chair where the cat sat watching the proceedings. "Me and Mac will be fine. It will take time, but I now know Cam will be there when it's my time and that makes living without him so much easier. That and remembering all the wonderful things we shared." She picked up the big cat and held him close.

Jessica tried to step forward again, but he held her in place. "But can you live without being so sad."

Holly looked at him and then returned her gaze to Jessica. "Yes, I can. In fact, thanks to you, I can treasure what Cam and I had now without regret. I've learned so much from you. Now I'm anxious to see what tomorrow will bring." She smiled as she sat in the chair, the cat in her lap.

Duncan nodded slightly at Holly before Jessica turned a confused face to him. "I guess we're done then?"

He glanced over her shoulder at the clock. Three minutes. "Yes, we're done." He looked at Holly. "Thank you, lass. Goodbye."

Jessica waved goodbye as she obviously fought tears.

He brought her to the land where his ruined castle stood in Holly's time. Just far enough from Holly but no' too far to sap Jessica's strength. As they landed next to the one tower left standing, she barely noticed.

Fearful of letting her hand go, he pulled her toward him and touched her face. His fingers felt her cheek, but his thumb went through her chin. "Jessica, you have to let go of Holly."

"I know, I'm trying, but I'm worried about who will be her Spirit of Christmas Present. What if it's not a good match? What if—"

Duncan silenced her with a kiss, thankful he could still feel her lips. Once she responded to him, he pulled his mouth away and leaned his forehead lightly against hers. "Lass, Cameron is her husband. I think he knows best who would help Holly the most."

She gave him the barest of smiles. "You do have a point."

"Besides, I need you a whole lot more than Holly does."

She pulled her face back to stare at him. "You do?"

"Aye. I didn't realize it until we were on Loudon Hill and I tried to take you home with me. When you weren't able to come back to the afterlife, my world fell apart." He pulled her glasses off and gazed into her fading green eyes, trying to will her to understand how he felt.

She shook her head. "But you can't love anyone. You said so yourself."

"I was wrong. Cameron helped me remember an event in my life which is why I was away so long. I *did* love once. It came just before my death, which was why it was so easy to forget. But I *can* love."

She cocked her head as if afraid of what he'd say next. "And you love me?" Her voice was barely a whisper. Her hand in his started to fade. Aye, he did, she had to believe him, terror swept through him and with it a memory surfaced.

He jumped in the water. Fuck it was colder than the top of Ben Nevis.

The woman's screams had meaning now. "The baby! Oh my God, she's in there!"

The torrent propelled him downstream, but the bundle of white was being swept away faster. He struck out with strong strokes, gaining. He had to save her.

His daughter!

A swirling eddy caught the bundle slowing it up, but sucking it toward its middle. Just as the baby's head went under, Duncan grabbed it up and held it close to his neck. Its cries turned to little whimpers that buried themselves deep in his heart.

He looked downstream at the boulders cutting into the rushing waters. The burn had never seen such water before.

A long branch caught between two massive rocks was angled toward him. Duncan grabbed it, stopping his forward momentum. He inched his way closer to shore, his muscles barely moving over the branch as his whole body grew numb. He kept touching his child with his chin, to make sure he still had her.

The coachmen called out as he ran down the slippery embankment.

Just a little farther. He wanted to lift the baby up to the man, but he was afraid he'd lose his grip. "Take her."

The man bent over the raging water and pulled Duncan's daughter from him. "Get out of there."

Get out of where? Aye, the water. Duncan tried to move his arms farther up the branch. He couldn't be sure he was successful, but he felt his feet hit something. Ground? Hope kindled anew and he pushed his muscles to their utmost and pulled hard.

The branch gave way.

Duncan went under. He managed to get his head above water one more time before he sank again.

Blackness crowded in. He'd never see her grow up, but she was safe.

But she wasn't safe. He struggled to push away the darkness. "I love you. Jessica, I love you."

"Duncan, come back to me, please." Her voice was stronger. He refused to yield to oblivion. No' this time. He wanted to be with the one he loved.

"Duncan, please." Her voice was scratchy with desperation. "I love you too. You have to stay with me."

Joy burst inside him at her words and the darkness disappeared completely. Her worried face was clear with every phased particle in place.

"You love me?"

"Oh my, you scared me. Yes, I love you with all my heart. I have for a long time, but I didn't think you could."

He ran his hands over her shoulders and down her arms before cupping her head and pressing a gentle kiss to show her just how precious she was to him. He lifted his lips away and let his gaze roam over every inch of her face. "I didn't either, but Cameron helped me remember. I love you."

"Oh, Duncan." She wrapped her arms around his neck and gave him a kiss, but this one was not gentle.

Understanding her need to be together, he opened his mouth and invited her in. Even as their tongues played, he swept them away through space and time to Rossan Castle.

He grinned as he landed them in his tower room and she pulled away.

"What are you smiling about now?"

"You are back to being a Spirit Guide, lass."

She looked around the room. "I'm in your castle again?"

He nodded.

Her eyes watered and she solidified, her cranberry scent filling his nose with wanting. Her features stood out more when solid and he loved every detail. Quickly, he solidified as well.

She wrapped him in a hug and spoke to his chest where she lay her head. "Thank you."

He held her tight, his eyes misting at how close he'd come to losing the one he loved once again. "Thank *you*." Love welled inside his chest and a new concern rose. Would his strong emotion toward Jessica trigger the blackness?

Chapter Eleven

Duncan wanted Jessica in a whole new way. A need rose in him to show her exactly how much he loved her before he ceased to exist. If it was going to happen anyway, he had to risk the pain of disintegration to make love to her one last time.

He tipped her head up to look at him. "Jess, I want to make love to ye right now."

She grinned. "That works for me."

He smiled. "I hope ye dinna think of it as work."

"Not at all. Hey, wait." She pushed away from him.

"What is it?"

She looked around the room for the first time. "That bed."

"Aye. What of it?"

She moved her finger to the bridge of her nose but there were no glasses to push up. "Where are my glasses?"

He opened his hands to the sides. "You dinna need them to see. You've had perfect sight since you arrived in the afterlife. You just never realized it."

Her eyes widened. Then she squinted at him before her gaze roamed over his loose white shirt, purple- green-and-red kilt, and stocking feet. A smirk formed on her face. "Is it true what they say about what a man wears under his kilt?"

"And what is it they say, lass?"

She shook her head. "If you don't know, I'm not telling. I'll just have to find out for myself."

He winked. "I think that be a good idea." He took a step toward her.

"No wait." She put her hand out.

"What now?" His cock was already hardening, just thinking of being inside her.

"That bed, is that the one, I mean have you, I guess, I don't want to…"

His heart shimmied as he realized her concern. "Nay, I've no' taken another woman in that bed. I've never even had a woman in this room besides my mother. Only you."

Her relief was palpable.

He didn't need to tell her this wasn't his bedroom. He'd brought too many women into his bedroom. Jessica was special, far beyond what she could understand right now.

She wandered over to the large four-poster bed and touched the maroon and gold curtains tied back on one of the corners. Then she looked at the table next to the fireplace before returning her gaze to him. "This isn't your bedroom. You may sleep here on occasion, but it's not where you dress and go to sleep every night."

Blast, the woman was perceptive. "Nay, it isn't. This is the room I used when I wanted to be alone."

She raised an eyebrow at him, a lovely sight to see without the glasses she usually wore.

"You want to know why I wanted to be alone?"

She nodded.

"If I tell ye, will ye get undressed?"

Jessica unbuttoned her top button and then the next one.

His mouth went dry as he tried to remember what he'd promised her. Oh aye, why he used the room.

Two more buttons were set free.

His gazed riveted to the cleavage now tantalizing him. His cock hardened further.

The last buttons were let loose and Jessica threw her blouse over the chair next to the table. "Duncan, you were saying?"

"Aye, I came up here when I needed to get away from everyone."

Jessica pushed her skirt down and stepped out of it, then smirked. "That's usually what alone means."

Duncan forced himself to look away from her tantalizing body. "I came up here when I wanted to think and no' be happy all the time. I was a second son, which meant my older brother had the weight of the world on his shoulders, but I was free to enjoy life. That's why it was so disappointing when…" He swallowed, saying the words aloud harder than he expected.

Jessica's arms came around him from behind as she pressed herself against his back. "When what?"

He'd never admitted his thoughts to anyone before. "When I realized I would never find the right woman to share it with." He grasped her hands at his waist and held them. "I didn't know she hadn't been born yet."

Jessica sighed. "I'm not sure which of us was worse, you for thinking you would never find love or me for deluding myself into believing I had found it."

He opened her hands and turned around. She was naked and he sucked in a breath as he embraced her, her tart scent filling him with warmth. "And have you found it, Jess? Are you sure?"

She smiled up at him. "Yes, absolutely, positively, sure."

He lowered his head and brushed her lips with his. He'd meant it to be a gentle kiss, but as their tongues entwined, he lost himself in the heady feeling of the woman he loved.

Just as his heart swelled, he felt her hands moving up his back beneath his shirt. The sensation of her soft fingers splayed across his skin made his heartbeat pick up speed. He broke their kiss and ran his hands over her back, finally cupping her rounded ass and pulling her tight against his kilt-covered cock.

"Ouch." She tried to pull away. "What is that?"

He chuckled. He'd been so anxious to have her against him, he'd forgotten about his sporran. "Hold on, lass." Quickly, he unhooked it and threw it on the table behind her. Before she could turn around and investigate his accessories further, he pulled her back into his arms.

"Now what was I doing? Oh, aye." He grasped her naked ass and pulled her hips into him, pressing his erection behind the wool of his kilt, against her skin. It was frustrating and tantalizing at the same time.

"Oh, Duncan, you feel even harder when you're solid." Her hands came to his sides and she pulled at his shirt. "Please take this off. I want to feel you against me."

Within a second he had his shirt over his head and tossed onto the floor. "Is that better?"

She ran her hands over his pectorals and as her fingers brushed across his nipples, he sucked in his breath. The need to be inside her had him clenching his hands. He wanted this to be perfect for her, for them.

She licked at his stomach. "I think I need to taste every nook and cranny of these hard abs of yours."

"Abs?"

She licked again and he gritted his teeth to keep from picking her up and throwing her on the bed so he could take her.

"Abdominals. Those are what we call these muscles here." She licked again.

"Jess, if ye dinna stop, I'll have to enter ye right here on the table."

She stilled. Then the little minx looked behind her as if considering his idea.

He growled and threw her over his shoulder. "That's it. I canna wait another minute more."

She laughed as he tossed her on the soft quilt.

His heart leapt at the sound of her joy. He wanted to hear that laughter forever…or as long as he had. Sobering, he knelt on the bed.

She sat up and faced him, a devilish gleam in her eye. "So let's see exactly what a true Scotsman wears under his kilt.

Before he grasped her intent, her hand slipped beneath his tartan and took hold of his hard cock. His balls tightened at the feel of her warm hand clamping around him.

"Ah, so it *is* true. You wear nothing beneath. I'm so glad." Even as her hand held him, she leaned forward and licked his right nipple. Blast, his body couldn't grow any tighter.

"Jess, ye be playin' with fire."

She let go of him and pushed him to lie back. He acquiesced, more than a little curious as to what she was about.

"Ach, lass, so ye want to ride me do ye?"

Jessica shook her head. "I want to pleasure you."

He raised an eyebrow. "Do ye, now?"

She grinned as she scooted down the bed to kneel at his feet. Her naked body—a vision to behold—kept him enthralled. Her firm breasts had light-colored areolas that boasted large nipples, which were hard, proving she was anxious to have him inside her. Past her belly was the tiny tuft of blonde hair he remembered from Loudon Hill, but she was solid now and that much more enticing.

"Now, I want you to just lie there while I have my way with you."

Her smirk was too tantalizing to his heart. "So ye want me to lie here and simply accept the pleasures of Christmas Past?"

She laughed again. "That's right. I'm the Spirit of Christmas Past and I plan to provide you with so much pleasure, you won't be able to hold back."

His cock jumped beneath his kilt even as his body prepared for her challenge. "I have complete control over my desire, lass."

She licked her lips. "We'll see."

Duncan's gut tightened at her words. Blast. His cock was already painfully hard for her. Exactly how experienced was she?

Jessica still couldn't believe Mr. Distraction who'd become Mr. Obsession was now Mr. Soulmate. She was positive her existence couldn't get any better.

The man lying before her, bare chested in a kilt and socks, was her daydream. That he loved her, filled her with awe. She wanted to show him exactly how much she loved him. He spent his life bringing pleasure to people, and way too many women in particular. It was time he was on the receiving end.

She put her hands on his knees and grinned as his legs tensed beneath her palms. Oh, she'd make the man lose control sooner than he thought. She moved her fingers down to his socks and her right hand encountered something hard. Confused, she leaned forward and pulled out a short knife. "What is this for?"

Duncan grinned as he held out his hand. "For whatever I need it for. To defend myself, to eat with if I'm outside, or to cut ropes that I might tie your hands with when I have my way with ye."

Jessica's breath caught as her folds moistened. She'd never done anything like that before and was more than a bit shocked her body reacted like it did. She placed the blade in his hand. "I certainly don't need it." She smiled slyly. "You won't keep me from doing whatever I want, right?"

Duncan's grin faltered.

She congratulated herself on putting him in an interesting position.

Instead of answering her, he shrugged. But that was enough

for her to know her time in control was of limited duration. She better get started.

She tried to pull the sock down over Duncan's rock-hard calf, but it wouldn't budge. His chuckle had her glancing up at him. "Now what? Why can't I pull these down?"

"Have ye never undressed a Scotsman before?"

She gave him a look that made it clear his question was beyond ridiculous.

He stopped laughing at her and smiled, the love in his eyes turning her body to springtime slush.

"And glad I am that ye dinna have more experience." He lifted his arms and settled his hands beneath his head as if he wouldn't do a thing to help. "The socks are held up by garters underneath the fold where the purple flash is."

She had noticed the little strip of purple, but had thought it sewn to the sock. Lifting up the top of the folded sock, she found the garter and untied it. The flash came off with it, and she was able to easily pull down the sock. She took it off Duncan's foot and threw it to the side of the giant bed. Then she did the same with the other. When she finished, she looked at him, triumphant.

Duncan gazed at her like he was a starved bear and she a fresh salmon. She took a deep breath and licked her suddenly dry lips.

A low rumble came from Duncan's chest, but he didn't actually voice any thoughts. Her whole body tingled at the warning. He would only be patient for so long. She rethought her plan to undress him and instead moved her hands up his legs and under his kilt.

Purposefully, she bunched the material at his waist, his strong pine scent distracting her a moment before her gaze feasted on his cock and balls now in full view. Then she lowered her head and blew.

His cock jumped toward her. She didn't dare grin or look at Duncan for fear he'd stop her playtime. Instead, she lowered her lips to the head of his erection and kissed the top.

Duncan's thighs distracted her for a moment. They tensed, showing muscle definition like she'd only seen in pictures of bodybuilders. Shit, the man was honed. Having that strength at her command was a heady feeling, even if it was for only a few minutes.

She flicked her tongue out and encircled the entire ridge at his tip before encapsulating the head in her mouth. His cock was harder than stone, and she couldn't resist licking up the underside, tracing the veins that pulsed there.

Her opening wept at the knowledge she would soon have this beautiful specimen deep inside her and moisture seeped beyond her folds.

Daring a glance at him, she found his stare intense as he watched her mouth suck at only the top of his ready cock. She slowly let it glide into her mouth, watching as his abdominals turned to cliff ledges. Unable to resist, she raised her head and let the tip pop out of her mouth then leaned forward, brushing her nipple against his wet cock.

Duncan's hands swooped down from beneath his head, but stopped just shy of touching her.

Since he didn't grab her, she sucked on his tip again and then stroked it across her other breast, turning herself on far more than she'd planned. From the corner of her eye, she caught his hands making fists against the quilt.

All that strength, restrained, told her she did indeed play with fire, but in this case she couldn't wait to get burned. Leaving his cock, she licked her way up the center crease of his stomach, letting her body slide against him, the soft wool of his kilt stimulating her skin.

She flicked one of his nipples with her tongue before she pulled it between her teeth and rolled it.

His chest rose as he took a deep breath.

Taking that as a sign he liked it, she moved to his other nipple and flicked and rolled that one too. Then she slid her body upward until her moist folds glided along Duncan's erection and her nipples brushed across his chest before she kissed him.

Duncan's tongue thrust into her mouth the second her lips touched his and her heart soared. Reflexively, she pushed her pelvis against his cock, loving the feel of her labia spreading as she rocked against him.

He pushed his hips up, hitting her clit with his erection, and she moaned.

Duncan's hands wrapped around her as his growl filled her mouth and he spun her over onto her back.

She grasped the back of his head as he continued to plunder her mouth with his tongue and slid his cock against her clit.

When he pulled his lips away, she opened her eyes to look at him, not sure when she'd closed them. "That didn't take long." She couldn't help the smirk that formed on her lips or the intake of breath at his hot gaze.

He quirked a brow. "I dinna want to disappoint ye." He pushed his pelvis against hers. "Ye seemed so ready, I dinna want to make ye wait."

She lost her smile. "Please, Duncan, don't make me wait."

His nostrils flared as his blue eyes darkened to cobalt. "Nay, Jess. I won't." His hips lifted and the head of his cock slid down from her clit to her opening. Without hesitation, he pushed into her.

She tightened around his welcome intrusion as he forced her sheath to widen and take him completely. When he'd reached his hilt, he angled his hips slightly and pressed a bit farther, sending liquid pleasure through every vein in her body. She wrapped her legs around him, resting her heels on the wool that covered his taut ass. "I love you inside me."

He brushed a kiss across her lips. "I love ye."

She stared into his eyes, mesmerized by the depth of his feeling for her. "I love you with everything I am."

A soft grin lifted his lips. "I plan to take everything you are, right now."

Before the shivers of anticipation had swept through her body at his words, he moved. His cock slid out and pushed back in while his eyes remained on hers.

Determinedly, she kept her gaze focused on his as his cock pumped in and out of her, the speed increasing at very slow increments, building the waves of excitement enveloping her body.

The intensity strengthened and still he watched her, even as both their bodies rocked against the bed with his thrusts. Her exhilaration built, tightening her passage even as he forced it open for his return.

His hips shifted, and he brushed his pubic hair against her clit.

Her eyes closed as the sensations converged, pushing her toward a precipice of ecstasy.

Duncan's lips touched hers and she opened for him, clasping him to her as his tongue delved into her mouth. His chest crushed her breasts, pressing the rumpled kilt against her tummy while his cock rocked into her. Every part of her enveloped by him.

Taken. Loved. Pleasured. Her body erupted. Sweet bliss spread through her, sweeping her into pure joy, even as Duncan's shout echoed in her ears. She held on to him like a person drowning, unwilling to be separated from him even in her moment of rapture.

When her heart finally slowed enough to allow her steady breathing, she opened her eyes to find her true love gazing at her, a soft smile on his face.

"Ye enjoyed that, aye?"

She gave him a faint nod and raised her hand to touch his cheek. "How could I not? To have the man I love bring me to paradise with him is absolute heaven."

He blinked rapidly and turned his head to kiss her hand.

"Are you crying?" Her heart was complete mush that he could feel so much for her.

He shook his head, but still wouldn't look at her. "Nay, ye are imagining things."

Her heart grew full, more than willing to allow him to deny it. To take his mind from his embarrassment, she tightened her sheath around his cock still deep inside her, more than a little surprised by the spear of desire that shot to her core.

He looked at her with the seductive smile that was so him and her body tingled all over again. Already?

"Lass, I am sensing ye want more." He eyed her with so much promise in his gaze, she found herself anxious to see what else he had in his bag of sexual tricks.

She gazed at him from beneath her lashes. "I'm anxious to benefit from your vast experience, but I don't want to wear you out. I do realize you need a bit of time to recover." She turned her head away just slightly and glanced at him from the corner of her eye. "Maybe I should go below and find you some food to help you regain your strength?"

At first, Duncan frowned, his brows drawing together in confusion. Then he scowled before he broke into laughter.

His body's vibrations on hers along with the thrill of hearing his laugh, had her seriously ready for him again.

When he'd gained control over his humor, he shook his head at her then suddenly pulled out.

Her groan issued forth without any direction from her.

He moved to the end of bed and grabbed his socks. Did he really need to get dressed to go to the kitchen?

But he didn't put the socks on, instead he crawled up the bed and took one of her hands and kissed it. Then he licked her palm, sending tingles down her arm and straight to her breasts.

He stopped and stared at her hardened nipples, causing her

to squirm. She used her other hand to plump her breast. "This is your fault."

He chuckled as he grasped that hand in his and pulled it above her head next to the other one.

Heat pooled in her abdomen as he tied her hands together. "What are you doing?"

Ignoring her question, he leaned forward and pulled the rope holding the curtains back. In no time he'd tied it to headboard then tied the other end to her wrapped hands above her head.

The wool sock was soft against her skin, but when she tried to escape it, it wouldn't budge though the length did stretch a bit. "Duncan?" She tried not to sound too worried, but being tied was not within her realm of experience.

"Is that too tight, lass?"

"No, it's fine, but what are you doing?"

"I'm going to pleasure you until you can't move."

"Do you need to use ropes to do that?" Panic seeped into her voice, though she tried to control it.

His eyes widened and moved back to look in her eyes. "Lass, ye ken I would never hurt ye, right?"

Now that she had his full attention, she relaxed a little. "I know you wouldn't on purpose, but I've never done this before."

His eyes lit with excitement. "Then allow me to initiate ye. I promise ye will enjoy it. I have so much I want to teach ye."

His own excitement communicated itself to her body, but her mind was still skittish. "I don't know."

He grinned. "Ye do remember how to phase, right?"

She rolled her eyes. "Of course I d—Oh, right." Crap, she must look stupid. If she wanted to, she could just phase out of the ropes.

He grinned as he lowered his head and sucked one of her nipples into his mouth. At the zing of excitement that hit her core, she went to grasp his head in her hand, but she couldn't. The helpless feeling that flowed from her brain throughout her body spiked her desire twofold. Oh yes, she was definitely sold on all his experience now.

He started to nibble, and she arched into his mouth. He pulled at the hardened nub before letting it pop from between his teeth. "See?" He grinned, perfectly confident in his ability to please her.

Her lips went dry at the thought of all his experience being brought to use on her…while tied. "I do."

He stood at the end of the bed and unbelted his kilt. After unwrapping it and throwing it on the table, he faced her. His cock stood rigid.

She swallowed hard at the sight of him and the knowledge he was ready for her so soon. She just needed to be patient and see where he would bring her to next.

He crawled onto the bed like a lion, every sinewy muscle moving in concert and setting her heart to fluttering.

Duncan lay next to her on his side. "Ye are so bonnie, Jess. I canna believe ye are mine."

Her blood heated as his gaze roamed over her chest. "I can't believe you're mine, though I can't touch you to prove it." Maybe he would take the hint.

"Ye dinna need to prove it, but I do." He moved his hand across her stomach before cupping one breast. "I want to show ye the pleasure of surrender."

Jessica's folds thickened at his words and her body turned to jelly. "What if I don't want to surrender?"

His lips quirked. "Believe me, Jess. Ye do." Duncan moved his hand over her breast, and with one large finger circled her nipple, causing her areola to pucker. Then he flicked his finger across her hardened tip, which sent tingles racing straight to her core.

She tried to pull her hands down, but the soft wool held her tight.

Duncan left that breast to give the other the same attention, first teasing her nipple by circling it with one finger then flicking it, causing her sheath to tighten. Then he stuck his finger in his mouth, before rubbing it over her hard bud. When he blew across her nipple, she arched with desire, wanting more than anything for him to suck. As much as she wanted to pull him to her, she couldn't.

Duncan must have read her mind because he leaned over and licked her nipple, lapping it, circling it.

Her sheath moistened with need and she arched as far as she could, pushing her breast against his mouth. He opened his lips around it and sucked, hard.

She squeaked.

He let up on the suction and looked at her, her nipple still in his mouth.

She nodded at his unspoken question. Then she grasped the socks holding her wrists.

He returned his attention to her nipple and again sucked hard. Need shot through her and moisture flooded her folds. He let go suddenly and she relaxed in the bed, unaware she had arched her chest toward him.

After tickling her hard nipple with his tongue he moved to the other one. He held that breast firmly and lowered his mouth.

She held her breath, anxious for the spike of need, already addicted to his skill.

He closed his mouth over her and gently sucked.

She arched toward him, now wanting the hard suction he'd shown her he offered. Instead, the man loosed his lips from her breast and lapped at her nipple. She gritted her teeth to keep from asking him for what she wanted. Instead, she stared at the cloth covering overhead and focused on the tiny tingles coming from his tongue.

His mouth covered her nipple and sucked hard.

She would have come off the bed with pleasure if he didn't have one large hand splayed over her stomach. When he stopped all suction and looked at her, she pouted. "So not fair."

He smirked. "I'm in charge this time."

A deep fluttering started in her abdomen at his words. She was so screwed...literally, and thrilled by that. But if he knew she looked forward to it, would it be as fun? She shrugged as if it didn't really matter, knowing he'd take it as a challenge. "Do what you will." She gave an exaggerated sigh as if she didn't expect much.

"I plan to." His serious face caused her heart to miss a beat. Suddenly, she had a feeling she may not be up to all he planned. *I can always phase if I want.* The thought helped her relax.

As Duncan trailed his fingers across her rib cage, over her belly and into the tuft of hair on her mons, she held her breath. When his fingers dipped between her legs, past her clit, she tilted her pelvis toward his hand. He didn't disappoint as his finger found the wetness in her folds and brought it to cover her clit.

She spread her legs, hoping his finger would accept her invitation to dive inside her opening, but he didn't. His fingers continued to coat her clit as they circled it, causing her muscles to tense as her excitement built.

Desperate for release, she bent her knees, and gripping the rope above her hands, lifted her pelvis from the bed.

Duncan's hand immediately left her body and he shook his head. "It isna for ye to seek your pleasure, but to allow me to give it to ye."

She moaned. "But I'm so close."

"I ken, lass. I ken." His smile proved he was pleased with his abilities to bring her to the edge of an orgasm. "But ye need to let go."

She swallowed hard to keep from whining. Instead, she simply nodded.

Duncan smiled and lay down next to her again, only this time, he turned her on her side as well and pulled her body tight against him.

Feeling his erection press against her ass gave her some patience. If Duncan was hard, it shouldn't be too long before he would thrust inside her.

"I think I could play in bed with ye for a full day."

Just the thought of Duncan making love to her for an entire day had her sighing. "That sounds wonderful."

His hand found her breasts again. With her hands above her head, she was helpless to do anything as he rolled her nipples, one after the other, causing her sheath to constrict in pleasure. Back and forth he went, sending lightning from each nipple to her core with every roll then moving to the other breast and doing the same. It was sweet torture and her heart raced. Finally, she couldn't take any more, her sheath flooding with wetness. "Please, Duncan."

His hand didn't leave her. Instead, he continued to roll her nipples, one after the other without stopping, even as he whispered against her ear, "I am pleasing ye."

His breath brushed the sensitive skin of her neck and a shiver raced through her body. She took a deep breath, pressing her breast against his hand.

He stopped rolling and grasped her whole breast and gently kneaded it. The sudden lack of stimulation gave her a chance to recover her breaths, but her body was tense with need.

Duncan's hand moved down her stomach and over her mons again. But this time his finger didn't stop. It thrust straight into her opening and she sighed with the promise of release.

But that wasn't Duncan's plan. He cupped her mons with his palm and with his finger deep inside her, he pulled her pelvis against him, pressing her ass into his cock where it nestled between her cheeks. Then one of his legs hooked her leg against the bed, holding her immobile except for her other leg.

"Lass, I love everything about ye, including this delectable body. I want to bury my cock inside your wet passage and stay there for eternity."

His words sent her pulse racing again, but it was nothing compared to when his finger left her opening and circled her clit.

She bucked as sweet need coursed through her veins and centered at her core.

As his finger played against her clit, Duncan's cock rubbed against her ass. She held on to the rope holding her tied hands together as if it could keep her from being swept away by pure bliss.

Then Duncan moved himself lower and pushed her free leg up with his hand.

"I canna wait any longer to be inside ye."

Before the thrill of Duncan's need for her had settled in her consciousness, his cock penetrated her opening from behind and he thrust inside her, pushing her tight walls wide, pressing into her until he could go no farther.

Her breath caught at the sensation of finally being filled, but her relief was short-lived. Suddenly the feeling disappeared. How could that be when she hadn't moved? "Duncan, what ha—"

The fullness returned, surprising her and she squeaked.

"Do ye like that"

"What did you do?"

He chuckled against her back. "I phased my dick then solidified it again."

Her sheath contracted around him. "Oh wow. I didn't know anyone could phase just part of their body."

"I don't know if others can too. It's just something I experimented with after phasing became so easy. Do you like it?"

"Absolutely." She grinned as the fullness inside her vanished again. Breathless, she waited to feel the sudden intrusion, and then it came. "Oh."

Duncan's hand moved back to her clit and began its play again, only this time there was purpose to the pattern, sending shock after shock of pleasure pulsing into her core and tightening her passage around his cock.

Then there was nothing. He built her tension and suddenly her tightness was spread wide again. Her pleasure rebounded against him, revving her body faster and higher.

He held her tight to him, unmoving as he played her. She gripped the rope holding her hands over her head like a lifeline as her whole body tensed and her sheath tightened against nothing, preparing for release.

Duncan's fingers teased her clit, her nub striking sparks of need into her belly and spreading like a wildfire. Then without warning, Duncan's cock filled her a scant second before his hips pulled back and he slammed into her.

Her world exploded.

Duncan gritted his teeth as Jess's passage squeezed him and pulsed against him, pulling at his control. But he held on, focusing on his finger movement across her clit and holding her bucking hips against him.

As her breathing slowed to a more normal pattern, he grasped her about the waist and held her.

"That was amazing." Her voice came out scratchy, husky and she cleared her throat. "I have never experienced anything like that…ever."

He smiled with pride though she couldn't see him. "There is so much more I want you to experience."

Her breath caught. A telltale sign she was ready to explore all he could show her. If only he had eternity. His mind told him he was on borrowed time, but his heart refused to yield.

Pulling out from her wet warmth, he stifled a groan.

"Where are you going?" Her voice revealed her disappointment in their separation.

Good, because he couldn't hold back much longer. "I just need to untie ye." He moved up and quickly loosened the sock, allowing her hands to slide free.

She pulled them down and rolled her shoulders. "I didn't realize how exciting it could be, not to have the use of my hands."

He rolled her onto her stomach and massaged her shoulders, trying to ignore how close his cock was to her ass. "I am pleased you enjoyed it."

"Hmm, I enjoy this too."

His hands refused to remain on her shoulders and instead they drifted down her back, massaging as they went. When he finally reached her ass cheeks, he couldn't help massaging them as well. He forced his hands to move to her thighs, spreading them, revealing her moist entrance. He couldn't wait a second longer.

"I need you." His voice rasped with his craving.

"Then take me."

His body reacted to her words and primal instinct took over. Lifting her hips, he plunged into her opening.

Her sheath welcomed him, tightening around him when he reached her end. "Yesss."

Her hiss was his final undoing. He let his body claim her, rock into her as it was meant to, making her his. When she screamed her pleasure, his heart burst with love even as his seed flooded her core.

When her panting had slowed, he pulled out, her moan of disappointment a balm to his soul. It was so hard to believe she loved him in return.

He lay on his back and pulled her to cuddle against him, his emotions far too close to the surface for him to bury them.

She pushed herself up onto his chest and brushed her lips across his.

He gazed into her eyes, letting the depth of his feeling show.

"Duncan, are you all right?"

He blinked at the water stinging his eyes. "Aye. I just canna believe I found ye."

Jessica's own eyes teared up. "And I you, but we did, and just in time."

A shiver ran through his body. It had been too close. He hugged her to him, determined to continue touching her until he was taken away.

~~*~~

Jessica listened to the sound of Duncan's heartbeat, so steady it could put her to sleep as she lay with her head on his chest, but a question still floated in her mind. "Duncan?"

"Aye."

"You said you had loved once in your lifetime. Who was it?"

At his quiet chuckle, she lifted her head to look at him.

His arm squeezed her tight for a moment. "You aren't jealous are you, Jess?"

She shrugged, trying to appear unconcerned, but it did make her nervous. If he had loved and remembered that love, would he search the woman out in the afterlife now that he'd remembered?

He pushed her hair away from her face. "She was a bonny, wee thing. All she had to do was smile at me and I was smitten."

"Oh." She didn't like the sound of that.

His smile grew wider. "But I could watch her sleep for hours, no need for her to put forth any effort."

Okay, now he was just rubbing it in. She lifted herself up on one arm. "You're not making me feel better."

His laugh caught her off guard.

"Jess, there is no need for jealousy. The lass I loved was my baby daughter."

Oh wow, she'd never even thought about the possibility that he had children. Based on his lover boy ways, there were probably dozens. "Did your family accept her? I mean, you were never married so…"

His brows lowered and his face grew serious. "They better have."

"What do you mean?"

He lifted his chin, stretching his neck like he did when he wore the "blasted" t-shirt. "The first time I met my daughter I knew she was mine. The woman I had been with was no' the type to do what she did with me."

"You mean have sex?"

He frowned. "Aye. I was trying to spare your feelings."

"Don't. It happened in the past, while you were alive." She gave him an encouraging smile, not because she wanted details about his daughter's mother, but because she wanted to know about his daughter.

"The woman was widowed and when she found herself with child she moved away from her village. But once my daughter was born, she realized she couldn't support her on her meager income and sent for me."

He paused and a look of pure happiness filled his face. "She had named her Isabella. When I looked down on Bella's face and her little hand grasped my finger in her sleep, I knew she was mine."

The look on Duncan's face caused a lump to form in Jessica throat. He had so much love to give. Everyone, including herself, including him, had done him a disservice by accepting the Duncan he presented to the world, instead of looking deeper to the amazing man he was. "So you took her home?"

He blinked, obviously lost in his memory. "I wanted to, but first I had to tell my family, prepare a room and hire a nursemaid. Since my brother had yet to marry and have children, my parents were happy to have a little one. Of course, she wouldn't inherit anything, but she was to be given a sizeable dowry, so she could marry well." His brows lowered in concern.

"But you never got to see her marry, did you?"

"No. Once all was ready for Bella, I sent for her. She and her mother were almost at the castle. I was anxious and rode out to meet them at the bridge across the burn. But we'd had weeks of rain and as the carriage came along the road next to the overfull burn, the embankment gave out and the carriage tipped."

"Oh, no!" Jessica's heart ached, afraid to hear what befell little Bella.

Duncan squeezed her waist again, as if keeping her close helped him relive his memory, so she laid her head down again, but kept her gaze on his face.

"Bella's mother and the coachmen were thrown partially into the water, but Bella slipped from her mother's arms and into the raging burn." He looked down at Jessica. "I've only felt that kind of terror one other time in my existence and that was when you were fading into a ghost."

Her heart expanded with love and tears filled her eyes. "Please tell me you were able to save Bella like you saved me."

He touched her cheek with his knuckles. "Aye, I did. I jumped into the burn and lifted my fair Bella out of the freezing water and handed her to the coachman. But my body had gone numb and when the branch I held broke, I was swept away. I died saving her."

She lay her cheek against his chest and hugged him tight. Relieved and yet overwhelmed by the man who was now hers. "Now that you remember, will you contact her here? I think I'd like to meet her."

"Jess." He lifted her chin with his finger. "I would like to, but I don't think I will have time. I was almost taken when I saved you too, but I refused to go. I wanted more than anything to experience this love we have found. I promise you, it is not common."

"What do you mean you were almost taken?" She leveraged herself up to make sure he was serious. He was.

Duncan looked away. "I am no' sure how much time I have left."

"What do you mean? It's not like you're going to die and you are certainly not turning into a ghost."

The need in his gaze when he returned it to her took her breath away. "I want to stay with you for eternity, Jess. But..."

Now he was truly scaring her. "But what?"

A figure floated through the wall.

"Ack!" She dove under the covers as Cameron Douglas solidified.

Duncan sat up. "What are you doing here? We finished our assignment."

Cameron leaned against the bed post. "Almost."

A growl issued from Duncan and she glanced at him. He was seriously angry.

"I dinna give a faerie's ass if we haven't finished, ye canna float in here and scare Jessica."

"Actually, I can. You see, it's time for you to move on."

She sat up, pulling the quilt with her. "I don't think so. He's staying with me."

Duncan ran his hand down her arm. "It's all right, Jess."

"No, it isn't." She glared at Cameron. "Exactly where do you expect him to move on to?"

Duncan looked at Cameron. "Let me tell her." He turned back to her, but her heart was already breaking.

"Those 'headaches' I've had grew a lot worse. It was part of my soul ceasing to exist. I dinna want to go, though. Now that I have you, I want to stay with you."

"I certainly hope so." Cameron scowled. "Because she's going with you."

Duncan threw back the covers and had his hands around Cameron's neck before she could react. "Duncan!"

Cameron phased. Duncan did too but a split second behind, which gave Cameron the opportunity to escape. He backed up two steps, laughing as he held his hands out in front of him to ward off Duncan. "No, no, Duncan she's not going there with you."

Duncan halted in midstride, his hands fisted at his sides. "Explain yourself."

"I will if you just give me a chance." Cameron took a second to catch his breath. "You were right, you were ceasing to exist, but you won't anymore."

Jessica wasn't following. "Why?"

Cameron smiled. "Because you love him and he returns that love."

She looked at Duncan and he looked at her.

"May I?" Cameron indicated the chair by the table. At Duncan's nod, Cameron moved her clothes to the table and sat. "I'm sorry I couldn't tell you, but I have even more rules than Spirit Guides."

Duncan took the couple steps back that brought him to the end of the bed where he sat and she scooted next to him, entwining her hand with his.

Cameron continued. "Any soul on this plane is here because he or she has not come to terms with his or her life." He looked at her. "For you, it was your regret. So many cases you wished you could have helped. You even regretted the cases you didn't live to get."

She squirmed. He was right there.

"You also regretted at the same time not marrying the man you were in love with because you were so involved with your work."

"You mean the man I *thought* I was in love with. But that wasn't love. You made that far too clear in my visits with Holly."

Cameron did look sorry. "And you, my friend."

Duncan raised an eyebrow, clearly revealing his doubt about them being friends.

Cameron sighed. "I know I was hard on you, but I had to be. When I first met you, I thought you were an anomaly. You were not only the oldest soul here but you were also the one who didn't appear to have any issues with your life."

Duncan squeezed her hand, but didn't remove his gaze from Cameron.

"That made no sense. Then when you had the episode when you finally won the bet against me on the Rangers game, I knew something was wrong so I asked Remiel some pointed questions."

Duncan tensed. "You asked Remiel?"

"I did. I was that worried."

She couldn't contain her curiosity. "Who's Remiel?"

Duncan whispered in her ear, "He is an arch angel."

"Oh." She wasn't sure what to make of that. She hadn't realized angels were real. Then again, she was a newbie to the afterlife, so she cut herself some slack. "So what did you learn?"

"That Duncan's soul was disintegrating."

"What?" She looked at Duncan for confirmation and he gave the slightest nod. "That was your headaches?"

"Aye, but they were a tad more painful. They lessened when I phased, but then I started to drift apart. When your connection to Holly grew too strong, I was forced to solidify in order to discover where and when you two had gone. I found if I suffered the pain, the darkness stayed away."

Duncan turned to Cameron. "But when I was trying to save Jessica, I couldn't solidify on the living plane, yet the blackness disappeared."

Cameron nodded. "Yes, because you finally remembered that your one significant regret was not having loved, so when Jessica told you she loved you and you believed that, you came to terms with your life."

"So I'm no' in danger of disappearing forever?"

Cameron shook his head. "No, you're not."

"Does that mean I can search out my daughter?" Duncan squeezed her hand, his anxiousness clear.

"Yes." Cameron smiled. "In fact, both you and Jessica have attained peace."

She had? She searched for that feeling of needing to help and not being able to and didn't find it. Her wish to know love had been completely fulfilled by Duncan. She looked at this man from a totally different country and a totally different century and was awestruck they had ever found each other. "Wait, how did you know making Duncan my mentor would save him?"

Cameron shrugged. "I didn't, not for sure. But I'd seen the women he'd been with and none of them were like you, so I hoped. You were my only chance to save Duncan and your connection to my wife was the perfect way to help you understand your place among the living."

"But I almost turned into a ghost!"

Her supervisor had the grace to redden. "I admit, my plan wasn't perfect. I misjudged exactly how connected you were to your cases and overestimated Duncan's ability to charm you."

She glared at him a moment longer, but couldn't stay mad. In the end, she'd found peace and Duncan, or maybe it was the other way around. But she still had one question. "Duncan remembered how he died, but I thought we couldn't remember that."

Duncan looked down at her. "I was wrong. Because I couldn't remember, I assumed we weren't allowed to, but you can." He looked at Cameron. "Right?"

Cameron nodded.

"How did *I* die? I know I wasn't sick or anything. So it had to be an accident or some fluke event."

Cameron nodded.

Duncan leaned down and whispered in her ear, "He's not allowed to tell you."

"Oh." Jessica tightened her hold on the quilt. "I'm leaning toward accident, most likely a car accident because I was forever driving to clients apartments over half the state."

Again Cameron nodded.

She tried to focus. She could picture herself on a highway, maybe interstate 95. No, that didn't feel right. She got off the highway onto another road. "Yes, I was on a road but it was way off the highway, but still well tarred." She looked at Duncan. "Some of the roads I traveled were dirt. But this wasn't."

Again Cameron nodded.

"Oh, I remember thinking how beautiful it was. The evergreens everywhere. The only sign of civilization was the telephone poles along the side of the road and an occasional home or trailer."

Jessica stilled. "Telephone poles." She saw the pole come at her fast. "I drove into a telephone pole?"

Cameron grinned. "Yes, but why?"

She forced herself to envision the ride. What did she remember seeing? It wasn't that she was sleepy. She'd been very alert. She didn't want to hit an animal if it— "A bear. It was a bear." She looked up at Duncan. "It was a baby black bear and I swerved to avoid hitting it and I crashed into the telephone pole."

He grinned at her. "I didn't realize you helped animals as well as people."

She smiled as a tear fell down her cheek. "Did I avoid it?" She looked to Cameron.

"Yes, you did."

She took a deep breath as if a weight had been lifted off her shoulders. Everything made sense now. Everything was right. "Thank you. I feel so much better now that I know."

"I'm glad. And what about you, my friend?" Cameron raised one eyebrow. "Did you remember everything?"

Duncan nodded. "I did."

"What about Bella, Duncan's daughter?" She looked at the man she loved. "Do you want to know?"

He turned to Cameron, his voice quiet. "Can you tell me?"

"Yes, I can. Isabella Montgomerie married Robert Hamilton and they had a brood of little Hamiltons."

Jessica sensed the tension leave Duncan's body. "Do you know if she married for love?"

Cameron nodded. "Yes, she did. Her dowry allowed her the pick of the men in the area." He moved his gaze to Duncan. "You're sacrifice enabled her to have a long life."

Duncan nodded, but he didn't say a word.

Jessica squeezed his hand, too pleased for him. "I'm so glad we know now."

"That's why you can move on."

Duncan tensed. "What do you mean move on?"

Cameron stood and walked over to put his hand on Duncan's shoulder. "I mean that after all the time you have been here and helped others to find peace, the gates of paradise are now open to you, my friend. They are open to both of you. You may continue on together for eternity now."

Jessica felt the truth of his words in her heart and her eyes teared. She glanced at Duncan, who stared at Cameron in surprise before his own eyes watered and he stood.

"Thank you, Cameron. For helping me remember and forcing me to see the love that was in front of me." He gave Cameron a hug.

When the men separated, Cameron leaned down and kissed her on the cheek. "Thank you for all you did for my wife. I knew you could help."

She smiled through her tears. "She is a wonderful woman."

"Yes, she is." The sorrow that was so much a part of Cameron's spirit seemed to return full force. As if he sensed her need to help him he held out his hand and laughed. "Oh, no you don't. I'm perfectly happy to wait for Holly. You two go on."

Duncan pulled her out of the bed.

"Duncan, I have no clothes on!"

He grinned. "Ach, lass, where we're going we dinna need clothes. Besides, would ye rather spend eternity with me clothed or naked?" He gave her a devilish smile.

"Definitely naked."

"That's my Jess." He brushed her hair off her shoulders and pulled her against him. Then he tipped her head and gave her a heart-searing kiss.

Pure joy filled her heart as they drifted into paradise. "Oh, wow!"

Epilogue

Cameron's throat closed as Jessica and Duncan disappeared in a burst of light. As much as he envied them their happiness, he wouldn't want Holly with him any earlier than her time.

He frowned. He was the idiot who cut their time short among the living. It was right that he suffer. But for her, he wanted her to live a full life, not one tainted by sorrow. Jessica had done a lot to further that possibility. She definitely showed his wife not to regret his passing but treasure their time together. If only he could do the same.

He shook his head. That wasn't likely to happen anytime soon, but this wasn't about him. This was about Holly. In her next year, he would send her more spirits to further his plan to make it up to her for his foolishness.

And he knew exactly who to send.

Phasing, Cameron flew above the castle and headed for his office, but in midflight he changed course. It couldn't hurt too much if he visited Holly before dawn broke on Christmas day.

It was sweet torture to see her and speak to her, but he couldn't stay long. Their connection was too strong and he could easily go down the path Jessica had. But a couple minutes, maybe three. Just to let her know he'd be back next year. For him, it would be no more than a blink of an eye, but he knew Holly. She preferred anticipating an event over being surprised. She said it made it last longer.

He smiled as their house on the main street of Deervale came into view, the Christmas lights in the window a beacon in the small town. Next door, the One of Kind Christmas Shop was dark and would remain so through Hogmanay. They had agreed it was a much needed holiday. What would she do with her week?

He tried to dispel the sadness his thought brought with it. He checked the grandfather clock in the corner. Good, he arrived at 12:12 a.m. The clock would alert him on the quarter hour.

Holly sat in her chair staring at the tree, giving Mac a good petting. How he envied that cat. He floated toward the fireplace, not wanting to scare her, and the cat watched him with a look as if to say "About time you showed up."

He must be imagining things. "Holly?"

She did start a bit before she stood and stared at him as if she couldn't look at him long enough. "Cam."

His name on her lips was filled with a longing that echoed in his own heart. "I just had to come and make sure you were okay after your adventures with Jessica and Duncan."

She crossed her arms. "You should have given me a bit more instruction before leaving. I think I jeopardized Jessica. Is she okay?"

"Yes, she is fine and she's with Duncan now, forever. You did great, hen."

Her brown eyes softened and her arms dropped. "I miss you so much."

He floated closer. "I know. I miss you the same. That's why I came back. I wanted you to know I'm going to visit you again next Christmas Eve if you want me to."

"Oh yes!" Holly threw her arms around him, but they went right through and she fell on the floor.

He crouched next to her. "Love, are you okay?"

She pulled herself up to a kneeling position. "Yeah, I forgot. I was so used to being phased with—hey wait. You can phase me. If I'm phased then I can touch you."

If he hadn't been crouched near the floor, he would have doubled over by the pain her suggestion brought. As it was, he had to wave his arm to remain floating upright. "I want to with all my heart, but I can't."

Her eyes started to tear. "But why? Jessica phased me and gave me hugs."

He nodded. "I know. That's why we almost lost her to the ghost realm."

Holly sniffed before a gleam came into her eyes. "So if you were no longer a spirit but a ghost, you could haunt me for the rest of my life, right?"

His need to see her happy battled with his pride in her intelligence. "Yes, but then after you passed, I would be stuck here so we wouldn't be together for eternity."

She crossed her arms as she thought about that. Then she sighed, the sound so defeated, he almost gave in. But, unlike other cases he doled out, he'd watched Jessica's and Duncan's interactions with his wife and to see a spirit transitioning to a ghost had made him physically sick.

He was pleased Duncan had been able to save Jessica, though he was pretty sure he'd be scolded by Remiel for giving Duncan the hint about his death. But it was worth it to transition both of his case workers, and it had helped Holly too.

He stared at his wife. Maybe he shouldn't have come. He may have undone everything they'd accomplished.

"Holly, please don't be upset. If you get too sad when I come, I'll have to stay away."

Her gaze met his at that. "I'm not sad. I'm just bummed I can't touch you."

He stifled the urge to smile and pull her into his arms. It would do no good anyway. "Are you sure you want me to come back next year?"

"Absolutely." She wiggled her brows. "Just think, I have all year to decide what to wear."

He laughed. Her spirit buoying up his own. "I hope it doesn't cost too much."

She gave him a sly smile. "The less there is, the more the cost."

His gut tightened as her meaning dawned. He was definitely being tortured and deservedly so. "Hen, you don't play fair, but I will still look forward to seeing you." He uncurled himself from his crouched position.

Holly stood as well. "Do you have to go so soon?"

He glanced at the clock. "I do, but I will be back. Dream of me tonight?"

She smiled sadly. "Every night."

The clock began its quarter hour chime.

"Close your eyes, love."

She did as he said and he floated through her.

The scent and feel and essence of all that was Holly clung to him as he sped away. He smiled. Now to put the next part of his plan into motion.

The End

Read on for a preview of *Desires of Christmas Present*

CHAPTER ONE

Arrogant. Asshole.

Those were the only two words that came to mind when Coco Baker heard the name, Ian Fergusson. Taken separately or together, they described him to a tee. "I'm sorry, but there's no way I can work with Ian Fergusson." She gripped the back of the chair in front of her. The man pissed her off simply by existing.

She didn't know how he'd ever been chosen as a spirit guide. She couldn't believe that the Scottish snob had ever had to work a day in his life. From what she'd seen, he didn't get along with any of the other spirit guides…or other spirits for that matter. Telling live people how they should feel and act just didn't work, and she was positive that's how he did his job.

Cameron Douglas, her boss, shook his head, his sandy brown hair falling onto his forehead with the movement. "I need two of you on this case. It's too hard a task for just one."

Oh, that was fine. "I can work with someone else, or if you like, I can bow out and wait for the next case." She'd just have to make it up to whoever was unlucky enough to be assigned to work with Ian.

Cameron leaned forward, setting his large arms on his desk and clasping his hands in front of him. "I'm afraid I need you, in particular, on this case."

"Me?" Had he noticed her track record? She'd begun to think only the spirits who knew spirits ever got promoted.

"Yes, you. I need your special instinct."

She flushed. "You know about that?"

"I do. It's nothing to be ashamed of, and on this assignment it will be very important."

She dropped into the chair in front of her boss's desk. When she became a spirit, she was surprised to discover her ability to recognize soulmates was still with her, but only among the living. It had helped her succeed on more than one case, but it felt as if she cheated when she used it. "Does this assignment have to do with helping someone find their true love?"

"No. I'll explain as soon as Ian arrives."

Despite her dislike of the man, she looked forward to seeing him. It was a pity he was such an ass because his body was to die for. Not that she'd seen him in anything but nice clothes. Casual for that man was a polo shirt and slacks, but his broad shoulders, narrow waist and rounded ass filled it all out quite nicely.

She preferred casual, especially the flutter shirt she wore. The pink stripes went with the streak in her hair and the three-quarter, wide sleeves hid what she considered her large upper arms.

Cameron shifted in his seat, obviously growing impatient.

She didn't like uncomfortable silences, especially with her boss. "Since we're waiting, could you tell me if Mrs. Maxwell is doing any better? I know I helped her see that she could still celebrate Christmas even though she was in a wheelchair, but I didn't run into Joy since she got back. Did all go as planned?"

Cameron relaxed, his smile quick. "Mrs. Maxwell is doing very well. The three of you did an excellent job with her."

She'd really liked the old widow and could see that her true soulmate had passed away. It hadn't been easy finding the right people to visit so Mrs. Maxwell could see she still had a purpose in life and a reason to live. "I'm glad. That woman has so much love to give, it would be a pity for it to end too soon. I think mankind needs as many people like her as it can get."

"I agree." Cameron sighed. "Unfortunately, Christmas can be the time of year when those very people find it the most difficult to keep going."

Boy, he could say that again. She'd seen far too many cases like Mrs. Maxwell's since she'd become a spirit guide.

Ian held Lucy's tiny hand firmly as he flew them over the rooftops of Glasgow, her silence an oddity after all her chattering this night. When they landed back in her bedroom, he let go and knelt in front of her. "Do you understand now?"

The eight-year-old nodded. "I do. Thank you for showing me. I promise I will be strong and not let anyone bully me into thinking I'm worthless." She pressed her finger against her chest. "I'm worth a million pounds!"

He smiled. "That's right. And what about the bullies?"

Her wide smile dimmed. "I feel sorry for them. I didn't know."

"Come here." He opened his arms wide and Lucy stepped into them. Hugging her was a balm for his soul that wouldn't last, but he craved it nonetheless.

Her pudgy little arms finally released him, and there was a tear in her eye.

"Now, Pumpkin. No weeping. Remember you still have another visitor coming tonight."

Her face brightened immediately. "Will he be as braw as you?"

Ian chuckled. "I don't know. It could very well be a woman who can talk dresses and dolls with you."

"I want a braw man." She crossed her arms over her chest and frowned at him.

He lowered his brow. "Now Lucy, remember what I said about

how special you are. You don't want me to cancel the next spirit altogether, do you?"

Her eyes widened. "Oh, no." She grabbed his arm. "Please let the spirit come."

He kissed her on the tip of her nose before rising to his full height. "All right, Pumpkin. I'll send the next spirit. Now let's return you to normal."

She stood still with her arms wide. "I'm ready."

He placed his hand on her shoulder and unphased her, his physical connection with her at an end. "Now you crawl into bed and take a nap." He glanced at the clock. "Your next visitor will be here in an hour and you want to be fresh for your trip into the future."

She smiled and ran to her small bed. Scrambling into it, she pulled the covers up to her chin. "Can you kiss me goodbye?"

His heart swelled. "Of course." If it wasn't for his assignments, he probably would have faded into nothingness, like he'd heard some spirits had done.

Brushing Lucy's cheek with his hand, though she couldn't feel it, he bent and kissed her there.

"And this one." She turned her head and pointed to her other cheek.

He obediently kissed the other one.

"And here." She pointed to her nose and he chuckled.

"Okay, last one." He kissed her button nose. "Happy dreams."

She nodded and waved. "Bye."

He floated toward her ceiling and waved back.

Once above the roof, he headed for his supervisor's office, the warmth and peace of Lucy leaving him the faster he flew. A tiny flicker of hope remained, his craving for another case already urging him on.

With no time in the afterlife, he was outside Cameron's door in a moment. Opening it, he stepped inside.

Coco turned around in her chair. Ian Fergusson stood just inside the door. His tall, broad-shouldered physique looked hard beneath his golf shirt even while relaxed. His face was equally hard as were his steel grey eyes. His angular jaw and sharp nose with a slight hook downward would have been enough to warn anyone to stay away, and beneath his short red hair were equally sharp ears. Everything about him was unrelenting.

He looked down his nose at her before raising his gaze to Cameron who had stood at his entrance. "I was informed that you needed me for a case. I can come back when you're done."

Her boss held out his hand and smiled. "No, come in. You'll be working with Coco on this one."

Ian raised an eyebrow and strode forward to clasp Cameron's hand. "I was unaware you ever sent two spirit guides on one case. I have always worked alone. I complete my assignment successfully that way."

Cameron nodded as he sat again. "Please." He motioned toward the other chair.

"I'm good." Ian waved him off.

Coco gritted her teeth. That was so like him. He thought he was above them all and could do what he wanted. She turned her gaze to Cameron. "Why do you need two of us?"

Ian frowned. "Yes. I can't imagine a case so difficult that it takes two spirit guides."

A team player he was not, but she'd already known that.

Cameron studied her, then Ian. When his gaze drifted between them, it was obvious that whatever he was about to say was important. Finally, he spoke, but didn't make eye contact with either of them. "Your case is my wife."

Shocked, she sat forward in her chair. "Your wife? But I thought—"

Ian interrupted her. "I was of the understanding that we were not allowed to take assignments directly related to us."

Cameron's gaze moved to Ian. "We aren't. However, this case has been given approval by Remiel."

"I didn't realize special dispensation was possible."

Seriously? She swallowed an exasperated sigh. "That's exactly what Cameron just said." Dimwit. She shook her head at Ian.

He didn't even acknowledge her, his gaze riveted to Cameron.

Her boss stared Ian down, which gave her a certain amount of satisfaction. Cameron's voice was hard. "This is a unique circumstance, Ian."

Her new "partner" had the grace to back down. Shoot, how was she going to control him if he tried pulling that crap on her? Maybe she needed to channel Cameron's deep tones.

The silence grew awkward so she jumped in. "What can we do for your wife?"

Cameron finally stopped glowering at Ian. Maybe he didn't like her partner either. That had to suck to not like your own employee. When she was alive, she had times when just being nice to her fellow workers was tough.

"Holly has stopped her deep mourning thanks to the spirit guides I sent to her last Christmas, but she has failed to join the living. She goes to work and does her errands, but beyond that, she stays by herself. It's become worse with the Christmas season." Cameron paused. "It's critical that she begin to socialize again."

Ian nodded, but Coco wanted more. "If your wife has stopped her mourning, why is she not socializing? Do you know? That might help us with our approach."

"I believe it's because she doesn't want to intrude on other people's lives. She thinks everyone else has the perfect life. Also, people who have come into our shop have shown her pity and she hates that."

Coco could hear the pride in Cameron's voice. Rumors around the lounge had it that Cameron and Holly had one of those rare loves that only happen to one in a hundred couples. She'd seen many perfectly matched couples both while alive and in her new existence. If what her boss and his wife had once had was even better than that then she would do whatever it took to help Holly.

She glanced at Ian. He remained absolutely still, staring at Cameron. Did the man have no reaction? No feelings? His appearance seemed to grow more distinct, intense. She blinked. Nope. He was still a hard statue.

When she looked back at her boss, he was studying her, but he quickly moved his attention to Ian. "Do you have any questions?"

"Yes, one." He paused and spared her a brief look. "If you have Coco, who is quite capable of handling a case, then why do you need me to accompany her?"

Her mouth dropped open in astonishment. Was that a compliment from "Mr. Holier Than Thou"? The man did nothing but argue with her about anything and everything when they came into accidental contact with each other. Now he complimented her?

Cameron's mouth had opened and closed a couple times before he gave voice to his thoughts. "Coco, if you wouldn't mind, I'd like to talk to Ian alone."

She rose. "Of course. I'll drop in and see how Holly is." She looked at Ian. "If you are still on the case, just find me when you're ready."

"He will still be on the case." Cameron's hard tone sent a shiver down her spine. He was an easy going boss, not like her last one, but he did have a certain tone that made a person want to hightail it out of his office.

"Great." She didn't mean the word in any way, but she also didn't want to piss off Cameron. Phasing, she floated down through the floor, anxious to meet the woman who had captured her boss's heart.

Ian's gut rolled into a sturdy knot at Cameron's tone. Fuck. He'd been muddling along just fine in his afterlife up until now. The last thing he wanted to do was partner on a case with Coco.

Besides her curvy figure and hypnotizing amber eyes, her energy pulled at him like quicksand. When she threw her dark brown hair with the pink streak over her shoulder and flashed one of her brilliant smiles, he wanted to grab her to him and kiss her until they both lost consciousness from lack of air—if that were possible as a spirit. But to do that meant to feel again.

Feeling was out of the question.

"Ian." Cameron's voice had lost its edge.

There may be a way out of this after all. "Yes."

"Have a seat."

Needing to negotiate his release from the case, he acquiesced to set the right mood.

Cameron came around his desk and sat on the edge of it. "Complimenting Coco won't get you out of this assignment."

He raised his brow. "That was not my intent. I was simply stating a fact. A fact that would negate the need for me to accompany her."

His supervisor shook his head. "This is not about her capabilities. There's a good chance she may run into difficulties while on this case, and I need you there as back up...and you may just learn something about yourself."

Discover something about himself? He snorted quietly. There was nothing he didn't already know, and what he knew, he didn't like. "I thought this was about your wife?"

Cameron's face softened. "It is." He stood and stared down at him. "And it better not get messed up or there will be consequences."

Ian straightened his shoulders. "I don't intend to make any mistakes." He was good at what he did. The question was, how was he supposed to perform well with another spirit watching him? And not just any spirit. "If, as you say, you need two spirits, then perhaps a spirit other than myself would be more appropriate."

Cameron stiffened.

Ian braced himself. Making his supervisor angry wasn't the smartest action he could have taken, but then again, he was well used to being on the receiving end of disapproval. His father had made him an expert.

But Cameron didn't yell at him. Instead, the man put a hand on his shoulder. "I know you don't want to do this, but you have to. Only by combining yours and Coco's talents can my wife come to see that not all is as it appears."

A strange sense of peace filled Ian's soul at Cameron's touch and he stood up, dislodging the hand on his shoulder. "You are incorrect. I am happy to do whatever is required of me. Is there anything else I should know?"

"Yes." Cameron's hazel eyes turned almost green. "You cannot fail."

"I don't plan to."

Also by Lexi Post

Paranormal Romance

Masque
Passion's Poison
Passion of Sleepy Hollow
Heart of Frankenstein

Pleasures of Christmas Past
(A Christmas Carol Series: Book 1)
Desires of Christmas Present
(A Christmas Carol Series: Book 2)
Temptations of Christmas Future
(A Christmas Carol Series: Book 3)
One of A Kind Christmas
(A Christmas Carol Series: Book 4)

On Highland Time
(Time Weavers, Inc. Book 1)
A Pocket in Time
(Time Weavers, Inc. Book 2) *Coming in 2021*

Sci-fi Romance

Cruise into Eden
(The Eden Series: Book 1)
Unexpected Eden
(The Eden Series: Book 2)
Eden Discovered
(The Eden Series: Book 3)
Eden Revealed
(The Eden Series: Book 4)
Avenging Eden
(The Eden Series: Book 5)
Beast of Eden
(The Eden Series: Book 6)
Bound by Eden
(The Eden Series: Book 7) *Coming Soon*

Contemporary Cowboy Romance

Cowboys Never Fold
(Poker Flat Series: Book 1)
Cowboy's Match
(Poker Flat Series: Book 2)
Cowboy's Best Shot
(Poker Flat Series: Book 3)
Cowboy's Break
(Poker Flat Series: Book 4)
Wedding at Poker Flat
(Poker Flat Series: Book 5)

Christmas with Angel
(Poker Flat Series Book 2.5/Last Chance Series: Book 1)

Trace's Trouble
(Last Chance Series: Book 2)
Fletcher's Flame
(Last Chance Series: Book 3)
Logan's Luck
(Last Chance Series: Book 4)
Dillon's Dare
(Last Chance Series: Book 5)
Riley's Rescue
(Last Chance Series: Book 6)

Aloha Cowboy
(Island Cowboy Book 1)

Military Romance

When Love Chimes
(Broken Valor Series: Book 1)
Poisoned Honor
(Broken Valor Series: Book 2)

Lexi Post is a New York Times and USA Today best-selling author of erotic romance inspired by the classics. She spent years in higher education taking and teaching courses about the classical literature she loved. From Edgar Allan Poe's short story "The Masque of the Red Death" to Tolstoy's *War and Peace*, she's read, studied, and taught wonderful classics.

But Lexi's first love is romance novels. In an effort to marry her two first loves, she started writing erotic romance inspired by the classics and found she loved it. Lexi believes there's no end to the romantic inspiration she can find in great literature. Her books are known for being "erotic romance with a whole lot of story."

Lexi is living her own happily ever after with her husband and her cat in Florida. She makes her own ice cream every weekend, loves bright colors, and is never seen without a hat.

www.lexipostbooks.com